THE INCOMPLETE ENCHANTER IS BACK

in another hilarious misadventure in worlds where magic works, and the fastest man with a spell is the man who wins.

Harold Shea was fast—but not always accurate. When you're dealing with dragons, wizards, and angry Saracens with long swords, this can be dangerous. It can also be wildly funny—and is, as Shea fights and magicks his way out of

THE CASTLE OF IRON

D0057249

L. Sprague de Camp and Fletcher Pratt
The Castle of Iron

a science fantasy adventure

PYRAMID
BOOKS

444 Madison Avenue, New York 22, New York

THE CASTLE OF IRON,
by L. Sprague de Camp and Fletcher Pratt

A Pyramid Book, published by arrangement with
L. Sprague de Camp and Mrs. Fletcher Pratt

Pyramid edition: first printing, April 1962

DR. REED CHALMERS, PROFESSOR OF psy-
chology at the Garaden Hospital, worked out the theory of
the simultaneous existence of an infinity of possible worlds.
There was no reason, he held, why any one of these should
be more "real" than any other, except as impressions from
them were received by the observer. He believed that
transit from one of these worlds to another could be achieved
by manipulating the symbols of symbolic logic. Morcover,
some idea of the more accessible of these worlds could be
obtained from the myths and epics of the world in which
an experimenter lived—such compositions being the reflection,
in the individual consciousness, of actual conditions in the
other worlds, transmitted along the psychic bonds connecting
the possible forms of existence.

His brash young assistant, Harold Shea, set out to prove
Dr. Chalmers' theory experimentally by launching himself
into the world of Irish myth, but through one of those slight
errors unavoidable in the practical application of theoretical
science, found himself instead among the gods and giants of
the Norse Eddas.

When, after various hair-raising adventures, he returned
to his own space-time continuum, he discovered that a
certain Gertrude Mugler was determined to look after his
welfare on a permanent basis, and set forth again on his
travels, this time accompanied by Dr. Chalmers, who wished
to test out some theories of his own with regard to magic.
They chose the world of Spenser's *Faerie Queene*, again they
found adventures, and Shea was accidentally projected back
to his own world, this time accompanied by his girl, the
huntress Belphebe. Dr. Chalmers had formed an attach-
ment for a lady, Florimel, who was originally formed out of
snow by magical processes. He decided to remain in Faerie,
in the effort to provide her with genuine flesh and blood,
as is described in *The Incomplete Enchanter* (Pyramid
Book F-723).

CHAPTER 1

"LISTEN, CHUM," SAID THE ONE WHO BREATH-ed through his mouth, "You don't hafta kid us. We're the law, see? We'll pertect you both all right, but we can't do nothing unless we got facts to go on. You sure they haven't sent you no ransom note?"

Harold Shea ran a hand desperately through his hair. "I assure you, officer, there isn't the least possibility of a ransom note. Since it's a matter of paraphysics, she isn't even in this world."

The red-faced one said: "Now we're getting somewhere. Where'd you put her?"

"I didn't put her anywhere. Didn't have anything to do with it."

"You say she's dead but you don't know who done it, is that right?"

"No, I didn't say anything about her being dead. Matter of fact, she's probably much alive and having a fine time. She just isn't in this space-time continuum."

"That's just dandy," said the mouth-breather. "I think you better come down to the station-house with us. The lieutenant wants to see you."

"Do you mean I'm under arrest?" asked Shea.

The one with the red face looked at his partner, who nodded. "Just holding you for investigation, that's all."

"You're about as logical as the Da Derga! After all, it's my wife that's missing, and I feel worse about it than you could. Will you talk to a colleague of mine before you take me down there?"

The one who breathed through his mouth looked back at his companion. "I guess that's right, at that. We might get something."

Shea stood up and at once was patted from breast to hip with a flowing motion. "Nothing," said the red-faced one disappointedly. "Who's this friend of yours, and where do we find him?"

"I'll get him," said Shea.

"You'll get a poke in the puss. You just sit quiet and Pete will get him for you." The one with the red face motioned Shea back to his chair, and unlimbering an unpleasant-looking automatic pistol from his hip, sat down himself.

"Oh, all right. Ask for Dr. Walter Bayard in the next office."

"Go ahead, Pete," said the red-faced one.

The door closed. Shea viewed his visitor with wary distaste. A mild schizoid of the suspicious variety; an analysis might turn up something interesting. However, Shea had too many worries of his own to be much interested in uncovering a policeman's suppressed desire to do ballet-dancing.

The policeman regarded Shea stolidly for a while, then broke the silence. "Nice trophies you got there." He nodded towards a pair of Belphebe's arrows that hung on the wall. "Where'd you get 'em?"

"They're my wife's; she brought them from the land of Faerie. Matter of fact that's where she probably is."

"Okay; skip it." The cop shrugged. "I'd think you brain experts would start on yourselves . . ." His mouth gave a quirk at the strange disinclination of the prisoner to discuss things on a rational basis.

There were steps in the hall; the door opened to admit the one who breathed through his mouth, followed by big, blond, slow Walter Bayard and (of all the people Shea did not want to see) the junior psychologist of the Garaden Institute, Vaclav Polacek, otherwise known as "Votsy" or "the Rubber Czech."

"Walter!" cried Shea. "For God's sake will you—"

"Shut up, Shea," said the red-faced one. "We'll do the talking." He swung ponderously toward Bayard. "Do you know this man's wife?"

"Belphebe of Faerie? Certainly."

"Know where she is?"

Bayard considered gravely. "Of my own knowledge, no. I assure you, however—"

Votsy's eye brightened, and he grabbed the arm of the one who breathed through his mouth. "Say! I know who could tell you—Doc Chalmers!"

The policemen exchanged glances again. "Who's he?"

Bayard cast a vexed glance at the junior. "As a matter of fact, Dr. Chalmers left only day before yesterday on a rather extended sabbatical, so I'm afraid he cannot be of much help. May I ask the nature of the difficulty?"

The red-faced one, quick on the trigger, said: "Day before yesterday, eh? That makes two of 'em. Know where he's gone?"

"Uh—uh—"

"Couldn't have gone off with this Mrs. Shea, could he?"

In spite of the situation there rose a unanimous laugh from Shea, Bayard, and Polacek. "All right," said the red-faced one, "she didn't. Now I'll ask you another one. Do you know anything about a picnic day before yesterday to Seneca Grove?"

"If you're asking whether I was there, no. I know there was a picnic."

The one who breathed through his mouth said: "I think he's covering up too, Jake. He talks like Snide Andy."

The red-faced one said: "Leave me handle this. Dr. Bayard, you're a physiologist just like Dr. Shea, here. Now how would you explain it in your own language that at this picnic Dr. Shea and his wife goes off in the woods, but only one of 'em comes back, and that one ain't this wife of his, and besides he goes around saying 'She's gone!' "

"I can explain it perfectly well," said Bayard, "though I don't know whether you will understand my explanation."

"Okay, suppose you come along too and tell it to the lieutenant. I'm getting a bellyful of this runaround. Bring him along, Pete."

Pete, the mouth-breather, reached for Bayard's elbow. The effect, however, was like touching the button that set off a nuclear reaction. As far as Pete, Bayard, Polacek, and Shea were concerned, the lights in the room went into a whirl of motion that became a gray-gleaming circle. They heard Jake's voice cry thinly: "No you don't!" with the accent at the end rising to a squeal, and felt rather than saw the orange, dahlia-shaped flame of the unpleasant automatic, but the bullet never touched any of them, for

Pmf!

The floor was cold beneath their feet.

Shea braced himself and looked around. Marble all right: there seemed to be miles of it in every direction stretching out in a tesselated pattern of black and white to where pillars leaped from it on every side, slender and graceful, supporting a series of horseshoe-shaped Moorish arches, and thence reaching back invisibly into the distance. The pillars were of some translucent substance that might be alabaster or even ice. Oriental, Shea thought.

"Listen," said Pete, "if you try to get away with this you'll go up for it all. This ain't like New York; they got a Lindbergh law in this state."

He had dropped Bayard's arm and was dragging out the twin of the red-faced cop's pistol. Shea said: "Don't bother shooting; it won't go off."

Bayard looked vexed. "Look here, Harold, have you been working some of your damned symbolic logic formulas on us?"

"Holy Saint Wenceslaus!" said Votsy, pointing. "Look there!"

From among the pillars that receded into the gloom a procession advanced. It was headed by four eunuchs— they must be that, loathsomely fat, grinning, wearing turbans on their heads and blue silk bloomers on their legs, each bearing a long curved sword. Behind came a file of Negroes, naked to the waist, with earrings, carrying a pile of cushions on their heads.

"You're under arrest!" said Pete, pointing the gun at Shea. He turned toward Polacek. "You want to preserve the law, don't you? Help me get him out of here."

The eunuchs went down on their knees and bumped their heads upon the pavement as the negroes, in perfect step, broke left and right to dump piles of cushions behind the four. Pete turned his head uncertainly, then turned back quickly as Shea sat. The reflex tightened Pete's finger on the gun, which gave out a loud click.

"I told you it wouldn't go off," said Shea. "Make yourself at home." He was the only one who had done so thus far; Polacek was turning his head round and round until it looked as though it might come off; Bayard was staring at Shea with an expression of furious bewilderment, and the policeman was clicking his pistol and working the slide in a futile manner between clicks. Behind the file of negroes another procession of butter-faced men emerged from the shadows of the colonnades, bearing an assortment of zithers, brass gongs, and eccentric-looking stringed instruments, to group themselves at one side.

"Nothing you can do about it. Honest," said Shea; then,

addressing himself to Bayard particularly: "You know about the theory of this, Walter. Sit down."

Bayard sank slowly into the pile of cushions. Polacek, bug-eyed, and Pete the cop, distrustfully, imitated him. One of the eunuchs pranced before the musicians, clapping his hands. Instantly they struck up an ear-wracking combination of shrieks, growls, groans, and howls, with a bearded vocalist, who seemed to have wildcats tearing at his entrails, raising his voice above all. Simultaneously, a door seemed to have opened somewhere among the darknesses behind the colonnades. A breeze fluttered the musicians' garments; underneath their squallings came the sound of distant, rushing waters.

"Cheer up," said Shea. "Here comes Room Service."

A dark-skinned dwarf, with a big aigrette held to his turban by an emerald clip, scuttled toward them, his arms filled with cushions. He flung them on the floor at the feet of the four, salaamed, and was gone. The caterwaulings of the music changed sharply, all the instruments together emitting seven high-pitched notes. Among the pillars, in the direction where the dwarf had disappeared, a flicker of motion appeared, grew, and developed into seven girls.

At least they appeared to be girls. They wore Oriental costumes, whose only resemblance to those pictured on calendars, however, lay in cut and color. Their long, loose pajamas were of the heaviest wool; so were the veils that covered all but seven pairs of black eyes and mops of black hair, while the bodices concealed everything above the waist. The howling of the musicians waxed as the girls cut a series of capers that could only by the remotest courtesy be called a dance.

"The vaudeville's corny," said Polacek, "but I'll take the one on the end."

"I'd hate to see him loose in a harem," said Bayard.

"I wouldn't," replied Polacek. "I wonder if she speaks English."

"You probably aren't speaking English yourself," said Shea. "Relax." Under those costumes it was hard to tell, but he was fairly certain that none of these was Belphebe.

The policeman, sitting bolt upright on a cushion, had stripped his gun in the space between his knees. Moreover he had gathered up the bullets that it had already disgorged, and with an expression of honest bewilderment was examining the firing-pin dents in their primers. Now he looked up.

"I don't know how you guys worked this," he said, "but I'm telling you to get us out of here or you're gonna do more time than Roosevelt was president."

"Wish I could," said Shea, "but Dr. Bayard will tell you it wasn't our doing that got you here."

"Then what *did* do it? Did you conk me on the head so now I'm dreaming? Or are we all dead? This sure don't look like the heaven they told me about at the First Methodist Church Sunday-school."

"Not exactly," said Shea, "but you're getting warm. You know how sometimes when you're dreaming you wonder whether you're dreaming or not?"

"Yeah."

"And how sometimes when something unusual happens to you when you're awake, you again wonder if you're awake? Well, we've discovered that the universe is something like that. There are a whole lot of different worlds, occupying the same space, and by mental operations you can change yourself from one to the other."

Pete shook his head as if to clear flies from it. "You mean you can go to Mars or somepin by just thinking about it?"

"Not quite. This isn't Mars; it's a world in a whole other universe, with different assumptions different from ours. What we do is fix our minds on those assumptions."

"Assump— O hell, if you say so I'll take your word. I'd think you was giving me a line, except . . ."

The seven had pranced off among the pillars. From the opposite direction another set of dancers emerged. They wore ankle-length trousers and loose embroidered coats with what might have been pairs of coffee-cups beneath. "Hi, Toots!" said Polacek tentatively. Scrambling to his feet he took two steps and grabbed for the nearest, who avoided him lightly without missing a step of her dance.

"Sit down, you damn fool!" barked Shea; the dancers swung past and began to retreat.

"How long d'you think this will keep up?" inquired Bayard. Shea shrugged. "No idea. Honest."

As though in answer, the orchestra changed beat and tune, with a violent banging from the strings and drums. From behind the disappearing dancers another pair of eunuchs stepped forward, bowed to the four, then faced each other and bowed again. Between them emerged four girls, each

11

with a small brass tray holding a fancy jar. Bayard gasped; Polacek whistled; the policeman ejaculated: "Mother of God!" The costumes of all were ample in cut but so thin they might better have not been there at all. The wearers were definitely mammals.

The girls sidled delicately towards their customers, bowed together with the precision of Rockettes, and flopped among the cushions at the feet of the four.

"You can't bribe me," growled Pete the cop. "This only gets you smart guys another charge. Indecent theatrical performance."

Keeping time to the music, each of the girls whipped the lid from her jar, stuck her finger into it, withdrew it covered with something yellow and gooey, and thrust it into her customer's face. Shea opened his mouth and got a fingerful of honey. He heard Bayard gag and cry "No!" and turned in time to see him try to avoid the finger. Pete the cop was dabbing a a honey-smeared face with his handkerchief, while his houri seemed determined to apply the stuff internally or externally.

"Better take it," advised Shea. "They're here to give it to us."

"You can't bribe me!" repeated Pete; and Walter said: "But I don't like sweets! I'd rather have beer and pretzels."

Out of the corner of his eye, Shea could see Polacek with one arm around his houri's neck, while with the other hand he conveyed finger-doses of honey to her mouth in exchange for those he received. He caught on fast.

Shea accepted another installment himself. "O moon of my delight," implored the policeman's girl, "is thy breast narrowed? Know that thou hast so infused my heart with love that I will rather drown in the ocean of mine own tears than see my lord dismayed. What shall his unworthy handmaiden do?"

"Ask her for something to drink," said Bayard, tentatively touching his tongue to the finger that was being offered him, and shuddering over the taste.

"Is this truly my lord's desire? To hear is to obey." She sat up and clapped her hands three times, then snuggled down again against the shrinking policeman's legs. He seemed past speech. The leader of the orchestra dropped his instrument and also clapped, and from among the pillars the dwarf who had brought the cushions came skipping forward again, this time with a big tray on which shone four elaborate silver flagons. Bayard raised himself to peer into the one set before him, then groaned.

"Milk! It needed just that to top off this mess. Who the Hell wants to go to Heaven? Good Lord!"

Shea, glancing across the head of his own houri, saw that if the liquid in the flagon was indeed milk, it was milk of a most peculiar kind, with small congealed lumps floating in it. Before he could experiment, Polacek shouted: "Holy smoke, you guys try this stuff! Best cocktail I ever tasted!"

The resemblance to a cocktail might be incidental, but the flavor was delicious and the potency unlimited. As Shea took a long draft he could feel a wave of warmth running down his gullet. He handed the flagon to his girl. "What do you call this drink, little one?"

She kissed the edge of the flagon where his lips had touched it and glanced at him archly. "O beloved youth, this is none other than the veritable Milk of Paradise."

Bayard had heard. "Paradise?" he cried. "Harold! Votsy! I'll bet you anything I know where we've landed. Don't you remember—

" '—For he on honey-dew hath fed
And drunk the milk of Paradise.'?"

"What you giving us?" demanded Pete the cop.

"This is Xanadu, Coleridge's Xanadu," explained Bayard.

" 'In Xanadu did Kubla Khan
A stately pleasure-dome decree,
Where Alph, the sacred river, ran—' "

"Alph! Alph!" The girls scrambled to their feet and bowed in the direction of the sound of running water.

"There you are," said Bayard. "Alph, supposedly based upon the legends about the river Alphaios in Greece—"

"That's it, all right," said Shea. "Listen, officer, I'm not responsible for this, and I don't know how we got here, but he's right. Wait a minute, though, Walter. This is a jam. Remember, the poem was unfinished; as far as I know we've landed in an incomplete space-time continuum, one that's fixed in a certain set of actions, like a phonograph needle stuck in one groove. This show is apt to keep right on going."

Bayard put both hands to his head, the policeman gibbered thickly, but Polacek waved an empty flagon. "Suits me," he cried happily, reaching for his girl again. "We'll do all right, won't we, babe?"

Just then the orchestra struck a strident note. The girl at whom Polacek had snatched dodged his arm, whipped up her tray with a smooth motion, and ran. Another group of seven dancing girls emerged from the pillars. One of them, apparently a soloist, carried a pair of short curved swords, which she began to brandish.

"But look here, Harold," said Bayard, "can't you do something about this? You've been telling us how good you were at magic in cosmoi where it works. Can't you get us off this goddam vaudeville circuit?"

"Yeh," said Pete the cop. "I'll tell you, Shea, I'll make a deal with you. Know feller in the D. A.'s office, and I'll get him to go eesh— easy with you on these here charges. Maybe, maybe, forget the indeshent performance one." The Milk of Paradise seemed to have warmed him no little.

"I can try," said Shea. "I don't know how it'll work with all this racket."

The cop heaved himself up unsteadily. "I can fix tha'," he said. In two bounds he was upon one of the astonished eunuchs, wrestling with him for his scimitar. The musicians stopped with a squeal and a murmur of voices; then one struck a gong, three times, ringingly. From among the pillars a whole parade of grim-looking janizaries advanced with long nasty spears in their hands, just as Shea wrested the scimitar from Pete. Bowing before the eunuch, Shea presented him his weapon, saying: "The humblest of your servants abases himself." Then he turned on Pete, whom Bayard was, with a little difficulty, restraining.

"You—utter—damned—jackass!" he said. "I don't care if you're the number one cop in Ohio; you can't get away with that here. How'd you like to see your head paraded around on the point of one of those pikes?"

Pete shook his head as if to clear it. "How—how could I see it if—"

"Or spend the rest of your life in a specially refrigerated cell?" Shea addressed Bayard: "Remember the 'Beware, beware!' and 'caves of ice' part? This paradise has got thorns in it; you take it the way they dish out to you, or you'll be sorry."

He led the way slowly back to the cushions. The janizaries had disappeared, and another file of dancers was coming out from among the pillars, this group specializing in bellybuttons. Pete the cop flung himself heavily into the cushions, and Walter Bayard sat down morosely.

"All right, you guys," said Shea, "try not to interrupt me while I give a whirl at a sorites. If there is something, c, such that the proposition *phi* concerning x is true when x is c but not otherwise, and c has the property *phi*, the term satisfying the proposition *phi* concerning —" His voice trailed off, and he sat with lips moving. Polacek watched him closely. Pete, head buried in his arms, murmured: "And me a married man!"

However, Shea's sorites was never completed. Through the domes building, far among the arches, rang the thunder of a cosmic voice—the kind of voice God might have used in telling the worshippers of the Golden Calf where to head in. It said: "Oh, goodness gracious, I do believe I've made a mistake!"

The voice was that of Dr. Reed Chalmers.

Shea and Polacek leaped to their feet. The musicians stopped; the dancers paused.

Then musicians, dancing girls, pillared hall began to go round, faster and faster, until they dissolved into a rioting whirl of color. The color faded to foggy gray. The gray threw up whorls that condensed into other colors, and faded into the outlines of another room, a smaller room, bare and utilitarian.

Shea and Polacek were facing a table. Behind it sat a short man and a pale, lovely, dark-haired girl. The man was Dr. Reed Chalmers. There were touches of black in the unruly gray hair that flowed from beneath the edges of a gaudy turban, and some of the lines were missing from his face.

He said: "I am glad to see you, Harold. I hoped—Oh, for goodness' sake, did I get Vaclav too?"

CHAPTER 2

"YEAH, YOU GOT ME," SAID POLACEK. "RIGHT away from a swell party. Walter, too."

Shea looked around. "But where is Walter? He was on those cushions—holy dewberries, Doc! He must be still back there in Xanadu with that cop, watching cootch dancers and eating honeydew. And he hates both of them!"

"Xanadu? Dear me, most unfortunate, most distressing." Chalmers fingered the papers before him. "I desired merely to establish contact with you, Harold, and I assure you the association of the others was quite accidental. I really don't know—"

Shea smiled crookedly. "I really don't know myself whether I ought to thank you or bawl you out, Doc. What have you done with Belphebe? You snatched her, too, didn't you? At least I hope so. She just disappeared while we were out on a picnic together, and they were going to arrest me for murdering her or kidnapping her or something."

"Yes—uh—there are certain difficulties." Chalmers's fingers moved nervously. "I am afraid there was rather a—uh—grave error on my part. I find the attitude of the police shocking. Though I do not think you need have worried about the legal complications. It would be well-nigh impossible to establish a *corpus delicti* under the circumstances."

"That's what you don't know, Doc. Gertrude Mugler was on the picnic, and she was the one who hollered copper when we went off on a walk together and I came back without her, nearly out of my mind because I didn't know whether some magician had hauled her back to Faerie. That woman could establish a *corpus delicti* or a society for boiling men in oil, and she would, too."

The pale girl made a small sound.

"Sorry," said Shea. "Lady Florimel, I present Vaclav Polacek, known in our country as the Rubber Czech."

"Hail, fair squire," said the girl. "The titles of your land are passing strange; yet not, methinks, stranger than that garb you bear."

Shea became conscious of a neat pin-stripe suit. "I might say the same thing about Sir Reed's headgear. What are you doing in that rig, what did you get me here for, and where are we?"

Chalmers said: "You display an unscientific tendency to confuse thought by the simultaneous consideration of different categories of information. Pray allow me to organize me thoughts and data. . . . Ahem. I presume it was you who employed the spell against magicians on Dolon, and in so doing projected yourself to our—er—point of departure? I confess I do not understand how you also projected the young lady. . . ."

"I had hold of her hand. We're married."

"My sincerest congratulations. I trust the union will prove happy and—er—fruitful. Your departure, you will remember, was attended by the destruction of the Chapter of Enchanters, and as a result I found myself faced by a problem rather beyond my powers. Namely, the transformation into a real person of a human simulacrum made of snow." He nodded in the direction of Florimel, who gazed at him adoringly. "I therefore—"

"Doctor, you got a chair?" asked Polacek.

"Vaclav, your interruptions are even more disturbing than Harold's. Kindly seat yourself on the floor and permit me to continue. Where was I? Ah, upon examination of available data, I was gratified to discover that there existed in Faerie the mental pattern of a universe whose space-time vector arrangement made it possible of attainment from that place by the familiar methods of symbolic logic. To wit, that of Ariosto's 'Orlando Furioso.' "

"Why should that be easy to reach?" inquired Shea.

"Ahem. I was about to explain. Lodovico Ariosto was an Italian poet, who wrote the 'Orlando Furioso' in what we should call the early sixteenth century. This work was considered the main source from which Spenser, a highly imitative writer, secured the ideas whence he produced 'The Faerie Queene.' Since each of these universes contains the same basic mental pattern, it is easy to perceive how transference from one to the other would be a relatively light task, and I felt confident that I would find here a number of experienced practitioners of magic. Vaclav, I perceive you are not following me."

"No," said Polacek from the floor, "and I don't believe Miss—Lady Florimel is either."

"It's not necessary that she should. For your benefit, however, I will explain that this similarity of basic mental pattern establishes, as it were, certain connective roads between the two universes, over which passage in our vehicle of symbolic logic can be achieved with a reasonable certainty of reaching the desired destination."

Polacek felt in his pockets. "Anybody got a cigarette? I believe you if you say so, Doctor, but I still don't get why you had to send for Harold, and why we had to land in that cabaret."

Chalmers fussed again with the papers, uneasily. "The process was attended by—uh—certain inconveniences. I can only describe them by—taking things in order, if you will permit me to do so. To localize the matter, we are in the castle of the leading magician of the 'Furioso', Atlantès de Carena, in the Pyrennees, near the Franco-Spanish border. For your benefit, Vaclav, I should explain that these places are by no means the same as we should understand by the terms employed at—uh—let us say, the Garaden Institute."

"All right, but why jerk me back here?" asked Shea. "You might at least have asked me first."

"Surely, Harold, you realize that symbolic logic is not a thing that can be handled like a telephone. As a matter of fact, the inconveniences to which I referred had become so grave that there appeared to be no other course open to me. I may be mistaken. Working with Atlantès has been most interesting, most interesting. I have been granted the opportunity of correcting many of the principles of magic in view of the somewhat different laws that control it here.

"However, I feel that I owe this young lady here a certain duty." He indicated Florimel, and blushed as Polacek and Shea both snickered.

"Ah—Atlantès has been most coöperative, but I hope I am less easily impressed by an enchanter's affability than formerly. Not only has he been unable to accomplish anything for Florimel, but these people are also Mohammedans with somewhat—peculiar standards of morality. I have been led to the idea, amounting almost to an absolute conviction, that it would be necessary for me to provide additional protection for Florimel. As matters stand, or stood before I took the perhaps unwarranted liberty of—er—transporting you here, I was the only barrier between her and our I fear by no means well-disposed host."

"I don't get all of it," said Shea. "Why couldn't you just take her somewhere else?"

"But where, my dear Harold? That is the very nub of the difficulty. To return to our own universe would be to lose the young lady, since she is of magical origin, and there's no provision for magic in the mental pattern. It must be regarded as impossible, at least until she has attained complete humanity. It would be possible, of course, to attain the world of Dante, but I am not sure that the atmosphere of the *Inferno* would be conducive to the health of a person made of snow. Moreover, Atlantès is an extremely competent magician, quite capable of either following her to another place or of preventing her going."

"A most persistent, arrant lecher," said Florimel.

Chalmers patted her hand and beamed. "I feel I owe an apology to you, and to Vaclav. However, one of the functions of friendship is to permit occasional impositions in times of emergency. And I trust you will look upon me as a friend."

Polacek waved a hand. Shea said: "It's all right, Doc, and I'll be glad to help, especially since you brought Belphebe along, even if it did get me in trouble with the cops. Where is she, by the way?"

Chalmers became more embarrassed than ever. "That is—uh—the difficulty over which I owe you my sincerest apologies. It was undoubtedly due to an error of selectivity. Er, I had not intended to transport her from our universe at all. If you are familiar with the 'Furioso', Harold, you will remember that among Spenser's imitations from it was a character called Belphegor, the cognate of Belphebe. . . . When the young lady arrived, there was a certain amount of—uh—confusion of identity, as it were, with the result, the unfortunate result, that she has no memory of another name or a previous existence. At the present moment I really cannot say where she is, except that she is undoubtedly in this universe."

"Do you mean to tell me that my own wife doesn't even know me?" yelped Shea.

"I fear not. I cannot express—"

"Don't try." Shea looked around the room gloomily. "I've got to find her. She may be in trouble."

"I don't think you need be apprehensive, Harold. The young lady is quite competent."

"Aye, marry, that she is," said Florimel. "She dealt Sir Roger such a buffet as will make his head spin for long when he would have let her from going without the castle but the now. Be comforted, Sir Harold."

"Who is this Sir Roger, anyway?" Shea glowered.

"I think I had better introduce you to my—uh—your associates," said Chalmers, and stepped around the desk to open the door behind Shea and Polacek. The air held an unmistakable faint odor of olive-oil, and as they stepped across the threshold, their feet gave back a metallic ring from the floor.

"Ah, yes," said Chalmers. "Perhaps I omitted to mention the fact that this castle is constructed of iron. That also is attended by certain—uh—inconveniences. Will you come this way, gentlemen?"

Another passage branched from that into which they had committed themselves, and led down a ramp towards a pair of double doors, with an oil lamp hanging from chains and throwing but little light. As they approached the doors, Shea heard the wailing sound of an instrument theoretically musical, like those in Xanadu. Polacek's eye brightened as he ran his tongue between his lips. "Babes?" he asked.

Without answering, Chalmers waved his hand at the doors, which swung open smoothly. They were looking at the backs of a pair of Arab-dressed musicians squatting on the floor, one blowing into a tootle-pipe, the other slowly tapping with his fingertips a drum about four inches in diameter. Beyond, a slinky dark girl in gauzy drapes revolved in the paces of a slow dance.

Beyond her again a dozen or more men were visible in the dim light of more oil lamps, dressed in bright Oriental costumes that seemed to have been specially spotted with grease for the occasion. Sprawled upon cushions, they gazed at the dancer with unsmiling, languid interest, exchanging a word from time to time, and looking toward the farther end of the room, as though to take their cue from the man who sat there. He was bigger than the biggest of them, with the figure of a wrestler. His young face bore strong lines, but just now it showed a sulky, petulant expression. A dapper

20

little graybeard, like a brown mouse, was whispering some-thing into his ear to the accompaniment of fierce gestures.

He glanced up at the sound of the visitors' feet on the floor and trotted toward them. He bowed low before Chal-mers. "The peace of God be with you." He bowed again. "Who be these lords?" He bowed a third time.

Chalmers returned one of the bows, "Let no less peace be with you, most magical lord of Carena. These are—uh—lords of my own country. Sir Harold de Shea, and the esquire Vaclav Polacek."

"Oh, day of good luck!" exclaimed Atlantès de Carena, bobbing up and down like a ship in a storm. "O day of Allah's grace that has brought two mighty lords of the Franks for these poor eyes to feast upon!" Bow. "Doubtless it is by some error that you have come to so poor a hovel, but in that error I am honored." Bow. "Ho! Let the best rooms be swept out and new ceremonial garments be prepared for Sir Harold de Shea and the squire Vaclav, for these be veritably the bringers of benisons." Bow.

Shea and Polacek kept up with the first two or three bows, but gave it up as the pace threatened to make them dizzy. Apparently satisfied that he had achieved something, the little brown man took each by the hand and led them around the circle where introductions and bows were repeated as though each man they encountered could not have heard what was said to the rest. There were Lord Mosco, the Amir Thrasy, Sir Audibrad—this last one in medieval European doublet and hose, without turban—and two or three more. In the intervals Polacek kept twisting his head to watch the dancer, until, at about the third introduction, Atlantès noticed.

"You desire this handmaid, noble lord?" he said. "By Al-lah, she is worth not less than a hundred pieces of gold, but you shall have her to your concubine, provided only that our Roger, for whom all things are done, puts not his claim upon her. And you will find her a pearl unpierced, a filly unridden, a gem—"

Polacek's face was reddening. "Tell him *no!*" whispered Shea fiercely. "We can't afford to get mixed up in anything."

"But—"

"Tell him no."

Atlantès' eyes were fixed on them, and there seemed to be an expression of amusement behind the wispy beard. "Listen," said Polacek, "I'll talk to you about it later. Since I'm just new here, I'd like to see more of your castle before— enjoying your—uh—hospitality. And—uh—thanks anyway, your lordship."

"Hearing is obedience." His lordship led the way to the cushion that supported the sulky youth. "And here is the light of the world, the arm of Islam, the perfect paladin and cavalier of Carena, Roger."

The perfect paladin gave a bored grunt. "More Franks?" he said to Atlantès. "Are they of better omen than that red-haired wench whom the Frankish enchanter lately brought?" Shea stiffened and his heart gave a thump. However, the light of the world was addressing him. "Are ye the new tumbling jugglers my uncle promised? Though my heart is straight-ened, yet may it find ease in witnessing your tricks."

Shea looked at him coldly down his long nose. "Listen, funny-face, I've been made a knight by a better man than you are, and I don't like the way you talk about the 'red-haired wench'. If you'll come outside, I'll show you a few tricks."

Roger, surprisingly, broke into a smile of pure amiability. "By the beard of the Prophet (whom God sustain)," he said, "I had not thought to find a Frank so generous. For months have I slain no man, and my muscles rot from lack of practice. Let us then to the hand-play!"

"Lords! Light of my eyes! Coolth of my heart!" Atlantès bubbled. "You have no need of another death and know well that a doom lies on it that there be none in this castle, and more, these be my noble lords and guests, fellow-magicians, for whose life I would give my own. Come, sirs, let me show you to your quarters, which, though they be but pal-lets in a corner, are yet as good as Carena can offer. 'Take what I have,' said the Hajji, 'though it be but half a barley-cake.' "

He clucked on ahead of them like a motherly hen. The "pallets" in a corner turned out to be rooms the size of audi-toriums, elaborately hung with silks and furnished with in-laid wood. The rivetheads protruding from the iron plates of the walls and ceiling, however, reminded Shea of the interior of a warship.

Atlantès was soothing. "Coffee shall be brought you, and new garments. But in the name of Allah, magical sirs, let the voice of friendship avert the hand of disputation, and be not angry with the kinsman of your friend. Ah, lovely youth!" he brushed a hand past his eyes, and Shea was surprised to see a drop of genuine moisture glistening on it. "The glory of Cordova. I sometimes wonder that the perfumed Hamman bath does not freeze in despair of emulating such beauty. Would you credit it that such an one could think more on blood than on the breasts of a maiden?"

He bowed half a dozen times in rapid succession and disappeared.

CHAPTER 3

"FOR THE LOVE OF MIKE, HAROLD!" SAID Polacek, eyeing the voluminous robes with distaste. "Are we supposed to wear these nightshirts?"

"Why not? When in Rome, eat spaghetti. Besides, if you want to give any of the damsels around here the eye, you'll have to be in fashion."

"I suppose . . . That little wizard's a smart guy. Say, what's this, a scarf?"

Shea picked up a long red strip of textile. "I think it's your turban," he said. "You have to wind it around your head, something like this."

"Sure I get it," replied Polacek. He whipped his own turban around with nonchalant speed. Naturally it came apart in festoons around his neck, and another try yielded no better result. Shea's own more careful procedure stayed on but settled itself firmly in concealment of one ear, and with a tail that tickled his chin. Polacek laughed and made a face. "Guess we'll have to call for a tailor or wait till they dish out some real hats."

Shea frowned. "Look here, Votsy, take it easy, will you. You'll simply have to be less cocky around a place like this if you don't want to get all our throats cut."

Polacek jagged up an eyebrow. "Hairbreadth Harry telling me not to be so cocky? Getting married has made a different man out of you, all right. Speaking of which, what are the rules around this joint? I'd like to take Atlantès up on his offer and pitch a little woo at that dancer. She's built like—"

The door was flung open with a clang by a man whose hairy, pendulous-eared head bore a startling identity to that of a Newfoundland dog. Without giving time for stares, he barked: "Lord Roger!" and stood aside to let the perfect paladin and cavalier stride in. Shea noticed he moved sur-

24

prisingly light for so big a man. He would be a dangerous antagonist.

"Oh, hello," he greeted the visitor coolly.

Polacek added: "Say, I'm a stranger here myself, but do you always walk in doors without knocking?"

"The lord is lord of his own saloons," said Roger, as though his name were Hohenzollern. He turned toward Shea. "It has reached me, oh man, that you are of knightly order, and I may without shame or hindrance take on myself the shedding of your blood. Yet since I am a warrior experienced, a person of prowess, it would be no more than just did I not offer to handicap myself, as by bearing no armor while you go armored in this combat when the wizards have lifted the death-doom from the castle."

If he had had the épée which served him so well in Faerie Shea would have returned the offer. Instead, he bowed: "Thanks. Nice of you. Tell me—do I understand that Atlantès is your uncle?"

"There is no other way to it." Roger tapped delicate fingers over a yawn. "Though he is rather like a grandmother, an old nanny with one eye, who holds all here from high sports for unmannerly diversions. Yet even this may be overcome if there be one with a will to warlike valor, who yet knows something of the placing and lifting of spells."

Shea was conscious of being keenly watched from behind the mask of boredom, and began to understand the purpose of the big man's visit, but it would not do to commit oneself too soon. He said: "Uh—huh. Say, tell me what's going on, will you? Sir Reed says Atlantès is worried about something. Are you expecting an attack by the Christian knights?"

"Ha! Christian knights I fear not, though it be all twelve paladins together." He flexed his muscles. "But of ifrits and enchantments know I nothing, and there is little joy here for any since the Duke Astolph stole the Atlantès' hippogriff."

Shea stood still, his eyes boring into Roger. "By the way, what was it that you were saying about a red-headed girl?"

Roger failed to notice the elaborate casualness of the question. "There is no glory but in Allah: it was but a few days since, during the time when Lord Dardinell was with us, when Atlantès and the other wizard, your friend, colluded to effect some great spell, with burnings and groans of evil spirits. There was nothing for it but that they must fetch from some far place this wench of ill-omen; well shaped, but unwomanly in garb, a huntress; and having red hair, which of all things more surely foretells some disaster, of which I fear the loss of the hippogriff is but the beginning. Have you met this unlucky one before?"

"My wife," said Shea.

"In the name of Allah! Are there no damsels of good augury in your land, that you must company with such an one? Doubtless she brought you a great dowry."

Without arguing the point Shea rushed on: "Has anything been heard of her since she left the castle?"

"It has reached me that one of the hunters saw her afoot in the mountains with Duke Astolph, a conjunction which brings a dread like midnight on the heart of my uncle, though what it may mean he knows not."

"Who's Duke Astolph, by the way?"

"Allah forgive your ignorance! He is one of the twelve whom the Christians (may they be accursed!) call paladins; yet a doughty fighter, to whom I look for the best of sport when I may measure blows with him, though he comes from an island far in the north, where it is so chill that men's faces turn blue, even though they be Franks."

Polacek asked: "Say, Roger, if you dislike Christians so much, how come you're wearing a Christian name?"

The perfect paladin went into such a grimace that for a moment Shea thought he was going to hit Votsy, but then Roger seemed to restrain himself with an effort. "Not for your question, which is the rudeness of a dog which lacks stripes," he said, "but to the good will of this knight who has offered me the sacrifice of his blood, will I answer. Learn, oh unguided one, that we of Carena are of too noble spirit to engage ourselves in the quarrels of princes, but seek honor under whatever banners may offer it, so that if the battle be hot, it matters not whose name it be fought in." Roger gave a snort, and looked at Polacek with unexpected keenness. "What said you but now of the slave-girl who danced for our entertainment?"

"Well," said Polacek, "Atlantès had—uh—made me an offer—very generous of him, I thought, and I was just saying that maybe for politeness I ought to take him up—"

"Enough, base-born," said Roger. "Learn that this castle and all in it were builded to my pleasure, and if it be my pleasure to take the damsel to concubine, there is no help for it but I must do so." He growled "Peace of God," and strolled out. The dog-headed man pulled the door to behind him.

Shea looked at the door. "You see, Votsy? Monkeying with guys like that is like telling Al Capone you don't like the color of his tie. Now let's get into those clothes and go see Doc. I noticed he solved the turban trouble and maybe he can help us."

He led the way down to Chalmers' apartment. The doctor was puttering away, chanting cheerfully:

> "We've a first-class assortment of magic;
>   And for raising a posthumous shade
> With effects that are comic or tragic,
>   There's no cheaper house in the trade.
> Love philter—we've quan—

What can I do for you, Harold?"

"These confounded cummerbunds." Shea watched as the doctor took Polacek's and adjusted it with quick, expert fingers, then began winding his own. "Look here, Roger says Belphebe's somewhere in the mountains around here. You've got to get me out of this place to look for her."

Chalmers frowned. "I fail to see the necessity for any immediate departure," he said. "The young woman impressed me as being admirably fitted to—uh—take care of herself. A perfect case of conjoined biological and psychological adaptation. And it would be most inopportune for you to leave at the present moment. We must look for the—uh—better manner of serving our united interests, and I am at present confronted with a serious problem—"

"Oh, Votsy can stay here and take care of her," said Shea.

"Vaclav is a bright young man, but I am afraid he is inclined toward irresponsibility," said Chalmers firmly, ignoring Polacek's squawk of protest. "Also, he has a—uh—deplorable weakness for the fair sex, not to mention that he lacks training in the most elementary details of magic. You, therefore, are the only person upon whom I can rely at present."

Shea grinned ruefully. "Okay," he said. "You knew you could get me with that argument. But you'll have to help me find Belphebe as soon as things are cleared up here."

"I shall be glad to help as far as I can, Harold, as soon as we have reasonable assurance of success in humanizing Florimel."

Shea turned his head to conceal the sparkle in his eye. Knowing how mulish Chalmers could get, he didn't attempt to argue. But he was a trained psychologist too, and he suspected it would transpire that he could best assist the transformation of Florimel at a distance from Castle Carena.

Polacek said: "Listen, you two. I might as well be some use around here. Why not show me how this magic works?"

"I had planned a series of talks on the subject," said Chalmers. "We will begin with the basic concepts, such as the distinction between sympathetic magic and sorcery. . . ."

"How about teaching me a couple of good stiff spells right now? Something I can use? You can get around to the heavy theory later, and I'll understand it better if I know the practical application."

"That would be unsound pedagogy," said Chalmers. "You should be aware that I am not one of those so-called progressivists who believes that the pupil absorbs best material presented in an unsystematic and confusing manner."

"But—but—I got a reason—"

"Yeah?" said Shea. "What's going on in that object you use for a brain, Votsy?"

"That's my business."

"No tell, no spell."

"Vaclav!" said Chalmers, in a monitory tone.

Polacek struggled with conflicting impulses for a few seconds. "It's that little dame," said he. "The dancer. Of course, ordinarily I wouldn't care—" (here Shea laughed raucously) "—not having really met her, but I won't stand for that big oaf telling me what to do. I thought if you gave me a couple of spells I could put on him—"

"No!" cried Shea and Chalmers together. The doctor said: "We are, I think, involved in—uh—sufficient difficulties already without further complicating our situation. I really do not know, for instance, how to avoid Atlantès' importunities with regard to the death-doom on the castle."

"The big guy mentioned something about that," said Polacek. "What is it?"

"It appears that at some time a spell was put upon this structure, I would conjecture when it was erected. The general effect is that if a killing should be performed within it, the building will collapse, though I will not weary you with the details, which are fantastically complicated. While I would normally be most willing to assist Atlantès, it now occurs to me that should this doom be lifted, our friend Roger will no longer be restrained from cutting you or Harold into fragments by way of sword-practice."

Shea muttered: "I'm not afraid of that stupid ox. I'll bet that all he knows is sabre-practice, if he knows that much."

"Perhaps not. Nevertheless, I should provide myself with a weapon. It would be most regrettable if our friendly association came to a sanguinary end. Moreover, permit me to remind you that as a married man you have incurred certain—uh—responsibilities."

Shea subsided, feeling guilty over having forgotten for some minutes that he was a married man.

"I still think you ought to teach me a couple of spells," said Polacek. "I won't turn Roger into a mud-turtle or anything like that, I promise, but I ought to have enough to protect myself."

"The amount of knowledge you could acquire so hastily would be of little value for self-protection," said Chalmers firmly. "The course will be imparted as I have outlined."

Polacek jumped up. "You two give me a pain. I'm going to see Atlantès. Maybe he knows a trick or two." He stormed out, banging the door metallicly.

Shea looked at Chalmers with concern on his long face. "Say, Doc, maybe I better go sit on his head, don't you think? He almost got into a jam with Roger already."

Chalmers shook his head. "I doubt whether Atlantès will impart enough magical information to enable our hasty young friend to—uh—jeopardize our safety, or for that matter, whether Vaclav can cause any particular damage in that quarter. In fact, it might be just as well if our host were allowed to gather the somewhat unfavorable impression of your—uh—characters that he is bound to form from contact with our associate. Now if you will lend a hand with this athanor, I shall finish compounding this mixture and we can retire for the night."

The last words set up a train of thought in Shea's mind that caused him to look more sharply at Chalmers. "Been rejuvenating yourself, haven't you?" he asked.

Chalmers flushed. "It seemed expedient, in view of the demands of my—uh—more active recent life. I was, as you perceive, conservative in my application of the formula, not wishing to become an adolescent by inadvertent over-dosage."

Shea grinned nastily as he bore a hand with the athanor. "The more fool you, Doc. Don't you know what the statistics show about adolescents?"

CHAPTER 4

HAROLD SHEA DREAMED HE WAS DROWNING in an ocean of olive-oil, too thick for swimming. Every time he reached the edge of an overhanging cliff and tried to pull himself out, a gigantic Roger with a cruel smile on his petulant face pushed him down with the butt of a lance.

He woke to see Vaclav Polacek on the edge of the other bed, holding a handkerchief to his nose. The whole place reeked with the stench of rancid oil. Shea reeled to the window, which was closed with some alabaster material. As he fumbled it open, a blast of chill but fresh air struck his face. He gulped. Beyond the castle battlements he could see the snowy crags of a range of mountains, pink in the early sun.

"What the hell?" said Shea, thoughts of some weird attempt at poisoning floating through his mind. Staying as near as he could to the open shutter, he struggled into the loose garments provided for him, and, without waiting to jockey the turban into position, made his way into the hall. There the odor was overpowering. As he turned the corner he bumped head-on into the Amir Thrasy, who was toddling along with a cut-open orange held under his nose.

"What the hell makes this stink, my noble friend?" asked Shea.

"Truly, sir, you are right and it comes from nowhere but the ultimate pits of the damned. But as the reason, it has been whispered to me that Atlantès (may flies nest in his ears!) has forgotten to renew his spell."

"What spell?"

"Verily, none other than that by which the smell of this oil is restrained within bonds, as the djann are bound by the seal of Solomon. It is certain that there is no spell against rusting, and, unless this castle be kept well oiled, there would be no help for it that it must be overthrown.

Yet is the spell for the sweetness of oil more fugitive than
a leaf in tempest, and must have renewal from time to
time, as . . ."

He stopped as Atlantès himself came bustling around a
corner of the corridor. "In the name of Allah, on whom be
praise!" he greeted them. "Most noble lords, forbear your
anger from your unworthy servant." He was bowing up and
down like a metronome. "Give me but the kerchief of your
pardon that my dread may be appeased and my heart
eased!" More bows. "I pray you, enlighten me with your
graciousness so far as to break fast with me. See, even now
the air grows purer than a spring of fresh water! And your
squire as well, glorious sir. Is the youth well?"

Shea's appetite, whatever it might normally have been,
had vanished under the shock of the olive-oil stench. Nevertheless he called to Polacek, and the Amir Thrasy fortunately
saved him the necessity of a reply.

"In sooth," said he, "our pains are borne lightly for the
sake of the pleasures to come, as we bore with joy the smell
of the corpses the day Lord Roger slew the two thousand
serfs at the gate of Pampelona, forgetting in his warlike fury
to leave any alive for the withdrawal of the bodies."

Their host conducted them to a breakfast consisting mainly
of stewed lamb with a sour, whitish liquid which Shea took
to be milk, rather noticeably unpasteurized. Roger, reclining
on cushions across the floor from the young psychologist,
gobbled horribly. There was no sign of Dr. Chalmers. When
the mirror of chivalry had finished his meal by sucking
leftovers from between his teeth, he stood up and said
meaningfully to Shea: "Will it please your honor to slash
at the pells, since under my uncle's ordnance we may not
slash at each other?"

"What's pells?" demanded Polacek.

Ignoring this question in a marked manner, Shea said:
"Delighted. But somebody will have to lend me a sword.
I came away so quickly I left mine home."

The pells of Castle Carena were a row of battered-looking
wooden posts in the courtyard. Beyond them, a couple of
men in castle-guards' livery were shooting at targets with
short, double-curved bows. Oddly enough, they had the
heads of baboons.

As Shea and Roger came out, Lord Mosco, a Saracen
so pudgy that he waddled, was facing the nearest pell

with a scimitar in one hand and a round shield on his other arm. He gave a blood-curdling whoop, leaped at the post light as a cat for all his bulk, and swung. Chips flew. Mosco went into a dance around the unoffending wood, slashing forehand with a drawing cut, and yelling at the top of his voice: "Allah-il-Allah! Mahound! Mahound!" He stopped suddenly and walked back to where the others stood in a little group. "My Lord Margéan, will you give me the balm of your word upon my performance?"

Margéan, in a kind of shapeless cap instead of a turban, and whose nose had once been well broken, said judicially: "I rate it but indifferent good. Twice you exposed your left side during the recovery, and the warcry did not ring. The foe is always the worse for a lusty shout in his ears."

Mosco sighed. "Blessed by the name of God," he said resignedly. "I fear I am a lost man unless protected by His angels or the arm of our champion. My lords, shall we not grace our eyes with the sight of these Frankish warriors?" There was a murmur of assent. "Now there is nothing for it but you must smite at these pells, squire."

"Better say you have a sprained wrist," muttered Shea.

But Polacek had his own ideas. "I'll get along. I've been watching him, haven't I? Where do I get one of these toad-choppers?"

The Amir Thrasy handed over his own somewhat battered and nicked scimitar. Polacek marched up to the pell, yelled: "Rah, rah, rah, Harvard!" and swung up in an underhand slash. However, he had misjudged the height of the pell; missed it completely, swung himself clear round the circle, tripped over his own feet, and had to clutch the post to keep from falling.

"That's my special attack," he explained with a shamefaced grin. "I make believe I'm gonna chop him, but instead I jump into a clinch and wrassle him down where I can really get at him."

Nobody seemed to feel the episode at all funny. Margéan's face expressed disdain, while the others looked away, all but Roger, who glanced at Shea to indicate that he was next.

Shea hefted Thrasy's weapon; aside from the nicks in the blade, it was altogether wrongly balanced for his type of work. "Has anybody got a straight sword I could borrow?" he asked.

Lord Margéan, who seemed to be some kind of coach, clapped his hands and called; a castle servant with the blubbering muzzle of a camel appeared with the desired weapon. Shea hefted it. The blade was straight enough, but the sword was as purely designed for cutting as the scimitars; no point whatever, the end rounded off, and the hilt made for small-handed man. The balance was better, though, and if the weapon was too heavy for a proper parry, it might do for a little lunging practice. Shea addressed himself to the post without shouting, did a simple disengage lunge, a disengage lunge with an advance, a lunge-and-remise. In five minutes he had worked up a healthy sweat, and was pleased to hear a murmur from the spectators, partly puzzlement and partly appreciation.

Margéan said: "Marry, sir knight, here's strange blade-play; yet methinks that with a Frankish sword you would even skewer one or two of your foes." And they began to argue about the merits of Shea's system: "Look you, lords, with a proper point like a spear you could even drive through the fine mail of Damascus. . . ." "Nay, I like not these newfangled tricks. . . ." "But see the reach it gives you. . . ." "Howsobeit, men will slash when excited. . . ." "Oho!" (to Sir Audibrad, who was awkwardly trying to imitate Shea's lunge) "it is plainly to be seen that the noble Sir Harold's tricks are not to be picked up in an evening over the coffee cups. . . ."

Only Roger looked contemptuous. Without preliminary words he strode up to the nearest pell, filled the castle-yard with a yell, and swung an enormous scimitar. *Chunk!* went the blade into the wood, and then quickly *chunk-chunk-chunk-chunk!* With the last blow, the upper half of the pell flew off, turning end over end. He swung round and grinned rather nastily at Shea.

Shea gulped. "Nice work, O Pearl of the Age."

Roger thrust his scimitar back into its scabbard and handed it to one of the servitors. "O Frank, this is but the tenth or the hundredth part of what would be seen if I stood in battle before a worthy antagonist. Not that you, son of an unfortunate, would be such; for you do but dance and foint like one of my uncle's entertainers."

While Shea and Polacek were giving themselves sketchy baths by standing in their washbowls and emptying the ewers over each other's heads, the latter asked: "What's the program for the rest of the day?"

"For most of them it'll be loafing all afternoon, I expect, and then Atlantès' floor-show in the evening."

"I should think those guys would get too bored to live!"

"Roger does. He wants to bash somebody, and I don't quite figure why Atlantès won't let him loose to do it. There's something funny going on besides just this business of the old guy making passes at Florimel. Wish I'd read the *Furioso*; I'd know better what we were up against. We have a date with Doc now, you know; some of that new theoretical stuff he's been working up. Ready?"

"Okay; let's go."

When they reached Chalmers' apartment there was more than a suspicion of the olive-oil smell that had awakened them. Chalmers was frowning.

"I am inclined to believe that the failure to renew the spell on the oil was not altogether an accident," he replied to Shea's question. "You will note that the odor persists here to a certain extent. Atlantès is extremely astute, and I have no doubt that he has become fully aware of Florimel's—uh—sensitivity. It really made the young lady quite ill."

Shea said: "Wonder why? Maybe the guy's a sadist. According to all the correlations, abnormal sex-patterns should be common in this Moslem society where they keep all respectable women locked up. Besides his personality reminds me of that sadist we used as a case study—you know the one I mean—that real-estate fellow the SPCA got after."

"You mean Van Gilder?" Chalmers shook his head. "In the first place those correlations you speak of are mostly guesswork. Besides, it would be unprecedented for any genuine sadist to seek his satisfactions by such indirect methods."

"You mean," said Polacek, "that a real sadist has gotta turn the thumbscrews himself?"

Chalmers nodded. "Or at least be present directing the operating. No, there are various explanations for elaborate bits of malevolent plotting of this type, but—uh—sadism is the last one to look for. An ulterior motive is inherently more probable."

"Such as?" said Shea.

"Such as—ah—if Atlantès hoped to force me to use a

counter-spell, which he would then watch and adapt to lifting the death-doom which he says overhangs this castle. Harold, please for that reason do not commit yourself to indulging Roger's penchant for mortal combat. One never knows when this conflict will materialize."

"I'm not afraid of him," said Shea, but without lightness.

"Looks to me like an awful lot of guys around here are anxious to get somebody bumped off," said Polacek. "Why don't you do something about it?"

"It is merely a matter of conducting oneself with ordinary prudence," said Chalmers firmly. "In an unexpressed contention of the type wherein we are engaged with the—uh —gentleman, the winner will undoubtedly be the party who longest restrains himself from ill-judged or impulsive action. Now, gentlemen, shall we begin?"

Half an hour later: ". . . the elementary principles of similarity and contagion," he was saying, "we shall proceed to the more practical applications of magic. First, the composition of spells. The normal spell consists of two components, which may be termed the verbal and the somatic. In the verbal section the consideration is whether the spell is to be based upon command of the materials at hand, or upon the invocation of a higher authority."

"That's a little different from the way you had it worked out before," said Shea.

"This is a somewhat different space-time continuum. I am trying to relate matters to our current problems, so pray do not interrupt. Now—uh—prosody is of the utmost importance if the first is the case. The verse should conform to the poetic conventions of the environment, to which the materials in question have become responsive. For instance in—uh—Asgard the verse, for maximum effectiveness, should be alliterative, whereas in Faerie it should be metrical and rhyming. In the world of Japanese mythology, on the other hand, the verse should comprise a fixed number of syllables in a certain—"

"But wouldn't any verse we made for the purpose naturally have the proper form?" asked Shea.

"It is possible. What I was about to say was that a certain—uh—minimum skill in versification is inseparable from the optimum results. That is why you, Harold, who have what might be called the literary or inspirational type of mind, often attain quite extraordinary effects—"

"Listen," said Polacek, "one of the troubles with this joint is that they're prohibitionists. You mean to say that if I made some passes and sang out:

"Beer, beer, beautiful beer,
Fill me right up with it,
Clear up to here!

I'd get a couple of seidels?"

"Václav!" said Chalmers sharply. "Pray give your attention to the matter in hand. If you were to perform so rash an act, you would almost certainly find yourself filled with the beverage in question, but I doubt whether your organs would retain it. The utmost precision of expression is necessary. Kindly observe that the doggerel you quoted demanded that you be filled with the liquid instead of having it to drink. Now, where was I? Ah—magic will thus, I fear, always remain to large extent an art, just as in my opinion psychiatry will as well. However, there is also the somatic element of the spell, subject to more precise regulation. There is some point in connection with this element that eludes me, and on which I shall be glad to have any light that observation of Atlantès by either of you, gentlemen, can throw. I refer to the very adroit manner in which he is able to employ spells as an instrumentality for teleportation of human beings or even those only quasi-human—"

Shea's mind wandered as Chalmers droned along. They had worked out most of this stuff in Faerie, with Belphebe—Belphebe! She must be the same as the Belphegor the doctor had mentioned. With the springy step and the freckles under her tan. The question of getting her back concerned the somatic element, of finding out how Atlantès . . .

An eruption from Polacek jerked Shea out of his daydream. The Rubber Czech was on his feet, exclaiming: "Sure, I get it, Doc. Let's take time out to do some lab work. Watch that cushion while I turn it into—"

"No!" shouted Shea and Chalmers together.

"Aw listen; can't you ever believe a guy can learn anything?"

"I remember," said Shea, "when you blew up the lab and almost killed yourself in sophomore chem, trying to make cacodyl. You stick around for some more lectures before you try enchanting even a mouse."

"Yeah, I know, but you can check me on each step, and I'm—"

The argument was squelched by the arrival of Florimel with: "I am somewhat more myself, my lord." But so, it turned out, was the lecture on magic. Shea wandered off to orient himself, while Chalmers undertook the difficult task of restraining Polacek.

CHAPTER 5

IT WAS CLEAR AND BRIGHT UPON THE BAT-tlements, and the air had the fine tang of a mountain climate. Around a corner where a turret gave both shelter from the breeze and exposure to the sun, Shea came upon Atlantès, busy with a scroll among long cushions. The little enchanter scrambled to his feet.

"O knight of the age, you are welcome. Will the friend of my friend have sherbets?"

"No thanks, noble host. I was just looking around, trying to find where things were in this place. You certainly have a fine layout."

"Alas, my lord, that it is no better. All things shall be done for him who eases the heart and broadens the bosom of Lord Roger."

"I wasn't aware that I'd done anything remarkable in that line. Will you have something special for him tonight?"

Atlantès snapped his fingers and shrugged. "Truly, I have nothing to set before you but seven virgins of Sericane, with faces like moons. All can play at the lute and sing, or hold converse in the law of the Prophet equal to Kasis, and the dealer who sold them to me declares they are sisters of a single birth, which is a very strange thing. Yet you, O auspicious one, will have seen wonders that are to this as the sun to the crescent moon."

He had tipped his head to one side and was watching out of the corner of one eye. What was he fishing for this time? Shea said: "I, O doubly auspicious one, have never seen anything like it. But tell me—" he let his voice fall "—your nephew, Lord Roger, will he like it as well as I? He seems restless."

The little man lifted his face toward the clear blue sky. "I testify that there is no god but God and I testify that

Mohammed is the Messenger of God! Of a truth Roger is no less than restless, and longs for battle as a strong horse for the race-course."

"Why not let him go fight one, then?"

Atlantès tapped himself once or twice on the sternum in a manner which Shea supposed was to entitle him to credit for having beaten his breast. "To you I will tell no less than the truth. Know, then, that there is a prophecy of which I have learned by my arts, that unless the wonder of the age and the son of my brother goes forth directly to battle and by the light of the full moon, he will be lost to Islam if he departs ten miles from Carena. Yet at present there is no war, nor is the moon full, and I must answer before Allah the just, the omnipotent, if he be condemned to Jehannum."

"Yeah, I see. You're in a tough spot all right."

The magician clawed at Shea's arm. "Yet it is well said: 'There is no door but a key may unlock it.' Verily, I have not seen my brother's son so content with his lot for many months as when he looked upon your exercises this morning. Doubtless you have a spell to preserve you from death by arms?"

It occurred to Shea that he had never in his life been more politely invited to let himself be killed. But he said: "What keeps Lord Roger here? If he's so keen on getting out and breaking somebody's head, why doesn't he just walk through the door?"

"In truth, that is a question asked with the answer already known, for it is not hidden from me that you are aware of the pentacles of opposition."

"I get it. This is a kind of gilded hoosegow. You don't think you can keep Sir Reed and me in that way, do you?"

This time Atlantes went through the formula of wringing his hands. "May dogs eat my flesh if I ever held such a thought! Nay, auspicious sir, should you wish to hunt in those mountains, where often I myself have had good sport when the sap of youth was in me, it would give pleasure to your slave to provide a hunter for company. And should you wish to sport with the light of Islam, the pentacles can be let down."

He certainly was persistent. "No thanks, not right now," said Shea.

The graybeard nudged him and chuckled lecherously. "Think well on it, my lord. It has reached my ears that there be maidens among the villages more dainty than gazelles, and not all hunting is done with the bow."

"No thanks, O fount of wisdom," said Shea again, wondering how much of his statement of the prophecy were true. "Right now I'm much more interested in Florimel's and Doc's—that is, Sir Reed's—project for her. Business before pleasure, you know. How are you coming along on that, by the way?

Atlantès went through his breast-beating routine again. "There is no god but God! It has not been revealed to me how this knot may be unloosed, though I have summoned up legions of the djann."

"Maybe I could help a little," said Shea. "I know a fair amount of magic, and once in a while I can do things that even Sir Reed doesn't pull off."

"In sooth, it were a greater wonder than burning water were matters otherwise, O master of magic. With joy and good-will will I summon you when the hour comes that you can aid me. Yet for the present there is no aid that can be given so great as that of the contentment of my brother's son."

Again! Would this little schemer ever let up trying to get Shea shortened by a head? Shea chose to ignore the last part of the remark. "Along what lines are you working? We might check results against each other."

"If it could be so, it were the delight of my heart and the expansion of my bosom. But it is unlawful for one of our religion to initiate other than true Muslims in the magical rites; were I to do so, you would instantly be torn in pieces by an ifrit stronger than a lion and with tusks three feet in length." The little man seemed to have had enough. He started for the stairs, the motion of his feet beneath the long robe making him look oddly like a centipede.

At the head of the stairs he turned to bow another farewell. Then a thought seemed to occur to him, for he held up a hand. "O auspicious sir," he called, "take warning. These peaks be ominous; very pillars of mischance. Let the hand of friendship avert the stroke of calamity, and in the name of Allah, I pray you, do not let down the pentacles nor go forth without help from me and mine."

The afternoon light was already beginning to throw panels of shadow among the higher summits. Shea walked on around the battlements, thinking of where Belphebe might be in this world, and longing for her high spirits. Damn Doc

Chalmers anyway for getting them into this jam! It was a jam, too. That farewell of Atlantès, though couched in a tone of appeal, came as close to a veiled threat as he had ever heard, Suppose he did lower the pentacles and walk out, what would the old goat do? Hardly let loose the wonder of the age on him. That would run against the prophecy—if there was a prophecy. Shea thought about the question as he picked his way past a clanging iron shot-tower, and reached the conclusion that the prophecy was probably quite real. Atlantès was clever enough to run a double bluff by mixing a piece of important truth with evasions and half-truths in order to steer an opponent away from the former.

The only thing he could count on, however, was that the magician was putting the heat on his guests in the matter of finding a cure for Roger's boredom. Shea considered the question for a moment. The big lug appeared to care for nothing but fighting; couldn't there be some way of meeting the wish vicariously? Back in Ohio, when children became problems along this line, the matter could be taken care of with books of adventure. That clearly wouldn't do here; or—and Shea mentally kicked himself for not thinking of it sooner—toy soldiers.

Certainly there ought to be somebody around Castle Carena with skill enough to carve passable small figures of fighting-men, and he and Chalmers between them should be able to animate them magically enough to enable them to serve as miniature armies. The thought of the perfect paladin ordering battalions of six-inch wooden knights about the courtyard struck him as so delightful that he slapped the edge of the battlement and laughed. At that moment someone plucked his sleeve.

It was one of the castle servants, this time with the head of a bird—a very large bird, with a great round head and a long bill like one of Tenniel's borogoves.

"What's the trouble?" asked Shea.

Although the creature seemed to understand, its only answer was to open the beak for a kind of whistling bark. It pulled at his arm insistently until he followed, looking over its shoulder from time to time and whistling encouragingly as it led him down the stairs, along one of the metal corridors, and left him face to face with Polacek.

"Hi, Harold," said the latter cheerfully, with the air of an inventor about to give birth to the atom-powered space ship. "Say, you guys need me around places like this. I got hold of one of those hobgoblins that will find all the stuff we want. The only trouble is I can't find her!"

"What stuff? Whom?"

"The little dark that did the dance last night. All I got is her name: Sumurrud, or something like that. And what kind of stuff do you think? Tonsil-oil, of course."

"You get around fast, don't you? Lead on to the liquor, but you're out of luck on the girl friend. If Roger hasn't got her in his room giving her the works just to spite you, Atlantès has probably sent her back where she came from by magic."

"For the love of St. Wenceslaus! I never thought of that." The Rubber Czech's face looked annoyed. "I'll cook up a spell on that guy that will make him—"

"No!"

"All right, how about this? Suppose I go to Atlantès right off the arm, and ask him can he send me that little number back to Ohio. With a build like hers—"

"No! We're in enough trouble now. You don't even know her, Votsy."

"But—"

Shea sighed. "For an educated man you've got the most proletarian sexual behavior-pattern—"

" 'Smatter with you; all worn out already?" said Polacek nastily, leading the way down a circular staircase in one of the castle towers. As this point in the argument was reached, so was a scullery, where the goblin, a purple-skinned object with an oversized head and spinkly little legs, was at his job of dishwashing. In one corner lay a large gaunt hound with a dish between his forepaws. The goblin held up a dirty plate, repeated a formula, and whistled. Instantly the dog reacted by licking the dish before him. As he did so the detritus disappeared from the plate held by the goblin.

"Guk!" said Polacek. "How do you like your dinner?"

Shea grinned. "Don't be squeamish. The stuff gets from the outside of the plate to the inside of the dog without touching a thing."

The goblin waddled over to them with a crablike gait. "Got it, Odoro?" asked Polacek with a wink. "He wants some too."

"Can get," said Odoro. "You got money, uh? Me want."

They went to Chalmers' laboratory for the money. At their knock there was a rustling from within, and when they entered, Florimel was some distance from Chalmers with her dress slightly rumpled and both of them looking hangdog. The doctor tendered some odd-looking square coins without comment.

As they made their way back to their own room, Shea laughed. "To see those two, you'd think it was a crime to hold a girl on your lap here."

"He's probably never done it before," remarked Polacek. "Well, he can have that human snowball if he wants her; I'll take that little Sumurrud. Did you know she was giving me the eye?"

The goblin joined them almost at once, producing from under one arm a small leather bottle wrapped in a ragged piece of discarded turban.

Polacek gave him some of the odd-looking coins, each of which the being tested with fang-like teeth. As he turned to go, Shea said: "Just a minute Odoro." He had taken hold of the bottle. "Your master is pretty tough about liquor, isn't he?"

"O yes, awful. Law of Prophet." Odoro touched a hand to his forehead.

"What would happen if he found out you had a supply and were selling it to people?"

The goblin shuddered. "Anathema, second class. Red-hot pincers inside." His grin vanished. "You no tell, no?"

"We'll see."

Odoro paled to lavender and made a shifting motion from one foot to the other that turned into a series of hops. "Oh, you no do! I do you boon! So do no nightly!" he squealed. "Here, you no want wine, you give me back."

He danced up to Shea, reaching. Shea held the bottle high over his head and did a snap-pass to Polacek, who caught it like a down-field end. "Easy, easy," said Shea. "Remember I'm a magician too, and I can turn you into a red ant if I want to. This is evidence. All I want is a little information, and if you give it to us you needn't worry about our telling anything."

"No got information," said Odoro sullenly. His eyes ran round and round the room from a swivelling head.

"No? Votsy, you go find Atlantès and tell him we've got a bootlegger here, while I keep an eye on—Oh, you don't want him to go? Maybe you do know a thing or two? I thought likely. Now then, is there a prophecy about Roger?"

"Yes—yes. Nasty prophecy. If he go out before full moon he join infidels, fight true believers. Inshallah!"

"Now, isn't that nice! All right, why doesn't Atlantès let Roger out just a little way? He's a wizard and would know how to keep him from going too far."

"Afraid Duke Astolph. He magician too; stole hippogriff."

"That clears up one point anyway. But look here, if Roger's so anxious to get out, why doesn't he just make it hot for Atlantès? Cut off his head or something?"

"Not know. Swear beard of Prophet, no know. Think Atlantès do something with—you know—mind—" Odoro pointed to his head— "drive Roger like horse. But Roger no got much mind, so hard to—uh—drive."

Shea laughed. "That's about what I thought. Give him another nickel, Votsy. You see, Odoro, you stick with us and you'll be all right. Now, what's Atlantès up to with Florimel?"

"Prophecy. Find in magic book."

"I daresay. What prophecy?"

"He lose Roger by woman knight, come on hippogriff."

Belphebe was out there somewhere in the hills, and so was the hippogriff. "But what does Florimel have to do with that?"

"Not know. Think maybe he change her shape with woman knight, burn her up, poof!"

"A fine kettle of fish. What kind of spell will he use?"

"Not know."

"You know about magic, don't you?"

"Not know that. Atlantès, he very good magician."

"Okay, Votsy, suppose you ask the very good magician to come—"

"Not know! Not know! Me ignorant!" wailed Odoro, beginning to hop again.

"Maybe he really doesn't know," suggested Polacek.

"Maybe. And maybe he gets a break for that crack about Roger. Run along, Odoro. You say nothing and we'll say nothing."

"Whew!" whistled Polacek when the door had closed behind the purple shape. "You certainly have got a nerve, Harold. With your luck and my brains—we get a drink."

Shea rummaged a couple of pewter cups from a low cabinet in the corner, uncorked the bottle, sniffed, and poured some of its contents into each cup. The wine was sweet and dark, nearly black, with something the flavor of port, though he judged the proof would be lower.

Shea sipped his, remarking with the air of an experienced conspirator: "You don't want to ask questions among the hired help without getting a hold on them somehow first. They may lie to you, or they may be souped up to report anything you ask to the boss. I think we've got this bozo playing on our team for the time being—but I don't like what he said about the deal Atlantès is cooking up."

"He means Belphebe, doesn't he?" said Polacek, holding out his cup for another drink.

"I'm afraid so. No, Votsy, we've got to hang onto some of this to keep Odoro in line. Besides, Atlantès would smell it on your breath a block away and know something wasn't kosher. We have to watch our step."

CHAPTER 6

IT WAS PLAIN THAT ROGER WAS NOT EN-
joying the party, although the seven virgins of Sericane were
giving him most of their attention. Harold Shea didn't know
that he altogether blamed the big bruiser. It was good second-
rate cabaret stuff, which might have been fairly enjoyable
had there been a comfortable place to sit, something to
smoke, and something to drink. Reed Chalmers had ex-
cused himself early and gone off to enjoy the company
of Florimel.

The dance went on. In the middle of a figure Roger suddenly stood up. "In the name of Allah! Oh, uncle, this is
not less than the vilest of your entertainments. My liver is
constricted, and I would broaden it by hunting bears
among the mountains."

Atlantès broke off his conversation with one of the lords
and began fluttering his hands, not aimlessly, but in the
passes of a magical formula. However, it had no visible effect
upon Roger, who trod firmly toward the door.

From beside Shea, Polacek said: "Say, I got an idea!"
and wriggled to his feet and followed. Nobody but the
seven girls seemed to mind the departure very much, even
Atlantès going on with his whispered conversation. But as
the number grew to a close Shea felt uneasy; Polacek had
too great a capacity for trouble to be left wandering around
the castle for very long with an idea in his head. He too
got up and strolled out into the corridor.

No sign of Roger or his friend. Shea ambled along the
hall and around a bend without seeing anything significant.
He was about to go back when his eye lighed on a side-
passage with a door at its end where a smoky light showed
the interlocked pentacles that protect magicians who deal
with devils. Atlantès' own laboratory!

47

In a moment the direction of his attention changed. The wizard was certainly well occupied, and if he did come looking for anybody it would be Roger. Shea stepped up to the marked door. No handle; and it did not move when he pushed it. Barred with a spell beyond doubt; but by this time he knew enough magic to deal with the situation. Reaching to his turban, he plucked from the brush that adorned its front a couple of stiff bristles, detached a thread from the hem of his aba, and tied the bristles together in the form of a cross. Holding this up to the door he whispered:

> "Pentacles far and pentacles near,
> I forthwith command you disappear!
> Shemhamphorash!"

He paused, hoping there was no basilisk on guard.

There was not. The room was long and lower than it seemed from the outside. A row of alembics and other magical apparatus lay ranged on a long table at one side, faintly reflecting the blue-white phosphorescent light thrown from the eyes of an owl and a crocodile which stood on a pair of shelves. The animals were quite immobile; evidently Atlantès' private system of lighting, though not one that would ever be popular with interior decorators. Along the shelf beneath them was a row of books, terminating in little compartments, each of which had a title on its attached tag.

The books had characters on their backs which Shea tried in vain to puzzle out until he realized that in this space-time continuum he would be unable to read English or any other language in which books were printed without special instruction. With the tags on the scrolls he fared better:

Ye Principalls of Magick with ye Conjuration of Dae-mons Superadded; Poisons Naturall; The Lawful Names of Allah; One Thousand Useful Curses; The Carpets of the Lesser Djann; Al Qa'sib's Manner of Magickal Transformations; . . .

Ah! This one might have what he was looking for. Shea pulled out the scroll and glanced at it in the eyelight of the animals. It seemed to be almost as strong on general theory as Chalmers himself, but little or nothing as to practical details. A glance showed him that, as might be expected, the scroll had neither table of contents nor index, and its style was so rambling that getting anything out of it would need a week's work.

Shea slipped the scroll back into its pigeonhole and turned to the rest of the room. If the enchanter were really trying to exchange Florimel's body for that of the menacing "woman knight" there ought to be traces of his labors about. However, the apparatus held no trace of filters, and the big scarred oak table beyond their bench lay bare. Atlantès was a neat sorcerer. Where would he keep his notebooks? Beyond the table was a stool and beyond that a low cabinet built into the wall. Like the outer door it had no handle, and as Shea bent closer he could see that its front was inscribed with pentacles. But at a touch it swung open, and Shea realized that his counter-spell must have let down barriers all over the castle. The thought that if there were any ifrits or demons abroad tonight they could get in and have themselves a hell of a fine time made him giggle under his breath.

The cabinet was deep, its shelves set back in, and in front of them a long straight sword hung in its scabbard from a hook. Probably an enchanted weapon, but the counter-spell would have taken care of that. Shea was about to reach past it toward the contents of the shelves when his ear caught the faint sound of a voice ordering the outer door to open.

In a flash Shea had snatched loose the sword and was on hands and knees behind the big table, which luckily had a decoration of carved wood reaching nearly to the floor.

The door opened. Shea could not see through the screening, but light from the corridor momentarily threw the shadow of a baboon's head across the wall on the side away from the door. The newcomer was one of Atlantès' servants, and a specially unappetizing member of the gang.

It stood in the doorway a moment, hesitant, as Shea himself had done. Then with the door swinging to behind it, it stepped confidently toward the bookshelves. But then it fell quiet—too quiet. Shea heard it sniff; sniff again, like the puffing of a toy engine. Of course it would possess a keener sense of smell than a man. The servant worked its way over to the table that held the alembics, tracing Shea's movements, just audible as its feet pressed the carpet. Shea could imagine the snouted head turning this way and that. . . . He gathered his muscles and shifted weight to bring his left hand free for the scabbarded weapon, planning in his mind how to snatch it out with the least lost motion.

The baboon-head reached the outer edge of the table, sniff, puff, sniff, puff, as loud as a locomotive in the oppressive silence.

Hell suddenly broke loose in the castle. A chorus of shouts and bangings echoed through the halls. The baboon-head paused for a moment, then ran to the door on almost soundless feet and out. Shea forced himself to count seven, then scrambled up and followed. The servitor had rounded the corner and the sound of its running still echoed metallically.

Shea turned toward the entertainment hall in the direction of the noise, pausing only in the side passage long enough to catch the sword on the belt beneath his flowing aba. It made him feel better.

As he approached the entertainment hall he realized that the noise was coming from beyond. He ran past to a big winding staircase, and from where it spread to a landing he could see Atlantès and his guests coming up with swords, maces, and even musical instruments, chasing a wolf the size of a heifer. It came straight toward Shea, but with its tail between its legs and looking utterly miserable.

Shea tried to dodge, then remembered the sword, but before he could dig it out of its hiding-place the creature was upon him. However, instead of leaping for his throat the wolf threw itself on the landing and rolled over, scrubbing its back along the iron floor. It waved its paws in the air, letting out an unwolflike "Wah-wah! Wah-wah!" Then it rolled back again and, keeping its belly to the floor, licked at Shea's shoes.

"Hey, wait a minute," said Shea to the crowding pursuers, who were trying to take swipes at the beast. "This is a rummy kind of wolf. It wants to be a pet. Atlantès, would you mind taking a look at it?"

The sorcerer dropped one of the singers' lutes and came forward. "Verily this is a most unfortunate rare creature, a wonder of wonders. Now shall you grant me room, Sir Harold." He squatted down and peered closely into the animal's eyes; it moaned. "There is no god but Allah! This is surely a werewolf. Oh, my lords, an evil hour has brought such a shape to Carena!" He reached to the neck of his robe and made a little tear in it. "Now I must seek by my arts to find how such a creature has passed our defenses. There is no doubt but that this is the work of the Christian enchanter, the paladin Malagigi, son of a hog and a she-dog, though I had heard of him imprisoned in Albracca." He looked round the circle. "My lords, we must seek a silver weapon for one of you to slay this brute, for being myself an enchanter I cannot."

Apparently silver weapons were in short supply. "O greatest of enchanters," advised Margéan, "shall we not affix silver monies to a wooden club and beat it to death?"

The wolf howled piteously. Chalmers, who had popped out of his own room at the sound of the commotion, had arrived in time to hear the last remarks. Now he put in a word: "Ahem—wouldn't it be the part of—uh—wisdom to attempt disenchanting the animal first? If I am correct in my understanding, it would then lose any previous invulnerability."

Atlantès bowed. "O fortunate hour that has brought your father's son among us, Sir Reed! This is nothing less than the truth. Yet I am but a stick set in the sand beside you in such matters. As your head lives, you shall now do this for us."

"Um—if we had some holy-water, it would a—uh—comparative uncomplicated matter, but I will try." Chalmers turned his back, put one hand to his chin, and meditated. "I am not sure the versification will prove adequate, but we shall see:

> "Wolf, wolf, wolf of the windy mountain,
>   Wolf of fear;
> I conjure you by the bitter fountain;
>   Disappear!"

His fingers moved rapidly. The wolf shuddered and turned into Vaclav Polacek rolling on the floor, clothes and all.

"Holy Saint Wenceslaus!" he cried, getting up. "Might as well shoot a man as scare him to death. Why didn't you lay off when I told you who I was?"

"You didn't tell us," said Shea.

"I did so. I kept saying, 'For the love of Mike, Harold, it's me, Votsy,' as clear as anything."

"Maybe it would have sounded like that to another wolf, but it didn't to us," replied Shea. "How did you get into that mess anyway? Did you run into this Malagigi that Atlantès is talking about?" There was a murmur of agreement through the group, as Atlantès' eyes darted back and forth.

"Well," said Polacek. He cleared his throat once or twice before he could get going. "It's like this, see? Roger isn't such a bad guy when you get to know him. He wanted to go hunting or something, and we were talking about it, but he said as how there was some kind of spell so he couldn't get out the door, and I said I'd been studying some magic, and so we went down there together, and he had the right dope; the door wouldn't open. Well, you see, I remembered those somatic passes Doc was talking about and made a few of them, and boy, the door flew open just like that!" He paused. Shea started a little, then hoped Atlantès hadn't noticed.

"Go on, Vaclav," said Chalmers severely.

"Well, then I figured I knew enough about magic to maybe—uh—get that babe back—you know, the one you were going to introduce me to." He appealed to Atlantès. "So I worked a little spell, just like you said, but it turned me into a wolf instead. I'm sorry I made so much trouble."

"Must be your Slavonic ancestry," said Shea. "The Czechs are full of werewolf stories, and—"

He had not noticed the gathering clouds on Atlantès' forehead. Now the storm burst. "Son of a dog!" he shouted at Polacek. "Where is the pride of chivalry, the noblest of his race, who is worth ten thousand such as you?"

"Why, he went out to do a little hunting, like I said," said Polacek. "He said he'd be back before morning with something good."

This time Atlantès really did beat his chest. "Ah, woe to me! The doom has stricken!" Then he swung around to the three Americans. "But as for you, Nazarene dogs, who have plotted against me by the hand of your servant while partaking of my bread and salt, you deserve nothing more than to be flayed alive and to have your bodies buried in a pit with the excrement of hogs!"

"Hey!" said Shea, reaching forward to take Atlantès by

the arm. "Those are fighting words where we come from. If you want to get tough about it—"

"Harold!" said Chalmers. "Let me handle this. We don't want—"

"We don't want anything to do with this thrip except to hand him a sock in the puss. D'you know what he's up to?"

Chalmers said: "Never mind, Harold. You have already informed me sufficiently. I'll defend—uh—myself and the young lady to any extent necessary."

Atlantès' fury had burned down to a glower. "O ill-omened sorcerers! Know that this castle was wholly established by the arts of which I am master, and within its walls I have such power that I could turn you to beetle-grubs in less time than the snapping of the fingers. Yet in the name of Allah, the omnipotent, the merciful, will I spare your lives to the undoing of the harm you have done, for it is written that once in his lifetime may the just man prefer mercy to justice without endangering his hope of paradise."

He extended both arms, closed his eyes, and cried in a high voice: *"Beshem hormots vahariman tesovev ha-esh, asher anena esh, et metzudat habsitel!"*

There was a whoosh and a buzz, like an electric fan in the adjoining room. Atlantès' permanent smile came back; so did his bow. "Behold, fellow practitioners of the noblest of the arts, if you will look beyond the walls of this castle, you will see it circled by an outer barbican of flame, sufficient to roast a sheep in less than a minute. For the hardiest of men to try to pass it the punishment would be no less than death. Yet if the Lady Florimel attempt it, who is a woman and yet no woman, she would leave no more memory than steam from the coffee-cup. My gracious mercy extends so far that the fire shall instantly be removed when by your arts you bring Lord Roger back; and I will add to that bags of jewels so great that three men can hardly carry them. The peace of the one true God be with you in your meditations."

He bowed again and turned his back. The lords looked sullenly at the three (except Audibrad, whose sympathies, judging from the fact that he was trying not to smirk, were evidently in the other direction) and Chalmers began to dither. "I—uh—am unsure whether I am sufficiently advanced in the science of apportation, which I had presumed something of a specialty—"

"S-st!" said Shea. "If magic doesn't work, I'll take a running jump through and go hunt Roger myself. I don't mind having my eyebrows singed a little."

Atlantès, who seemed to have sharper ears than a cat, turned back. "Learn, rash, youth," he said, "that the very marrow of your bones would be incinerated; and yet, of a truth, you say a thing I had not thought on; for it will be far easier to remove the Pearl of the Orient from thence to hither if he be found by human eyes than only by arts magical; and it will greatly pleasure my brother's son to cut your throat from ear to ear beyond these walls. Go, then; I undertake to pass you unharmed through the flame."

"I'd like to go, too," said Polacek. His expression showed that he did not look forward to a pleasant time at the castle after his venture into wolfishness.

"Go, then, and Allah give you neither peace nor a long life unless you bring my nephew home again." He turned away again, this time for keeps.

Shea found Chalmers looking at him keenly. The doctor said: "I wonder, Harold, if helping me and Florimel was your most important motive in offering to find Roger?"

Shea grinned. "It's the only one you know about officially, Doc."

CHAPTER 7

THE WHOLE CASTLE TURNED OUT TO SEE
Shea and Polacek off on their Roger-hunt the following
morning. During the evening, Chalmers had tried to establish
thought-contact with the peerless chevalier as a preliminary
to getting back by magical means, but he had been forced
to give up with the remark that Roger had about as few
thoughts as the human brain could hold. In any case there
seemed to be interference, either from Atlantès himself or
from the curtain of flame he had thrown around the castle,
so the job clearly devolved upon Chalmers' two juniors.

He did not believe that the threat of Atlantès' plan to
exchange the shapes of Florimel and the prophesied woman
knight represented an immediate danger. Perhaps later;
"But let us take first things first, Harold," he said cheerfully.
"I think I can profitably employ my time in study and in
attempting to establish communication with this Christian
sorcerer Malagigi. It was—uh—remiss of me not to have
thought of him before coming to Carena. I presume it
would be superfluous to express a wish for your good
fortune?"

Beyond the gate and a drawbridge over a dry ditch, the
flames rose in a wavering wall, obscuring the nearby peaks.
Shea could feel their heat on his face as he stood at the
break of the drawbridge while Atlantès dipped a finger in a
small bottle of oil and drew an isosceles triangle on his
forehead and then a right triangle over the first, muttering
a small spell as he did so. He repeated the process with
Polacek and with the chief huntsman of the castle, a broad-
shouldered, swarthy man named Echegaray. Atlantès was
all smiles as though they had had no hard words the previous
evening, although Shea overheard the other lords making up
a small pool as to who would find Roger and when.

Echegaray strode beside them towards the flame, a cross-bow over his shoulder. When he came to the magic barrier, however, he stopped and looked inquiringly at Shea. The flames streaked soundlessly far over their heads; the light was so intense that it hurt their eyes and looked altogether real and terrifying, though the grass from which the flames sprang seemed unharmed. Shea felt like stopping too, but with Echegaray watching and the eyes of the whole castle boring into his back—he threw out his chest and marched straight through. Two steps did it, and the fire only tingled.

For a moment his companions did not appear. Then there was a half-choked yell and Echegaray came through, drag-ging Polacek behind him. The hunter looked at Shea, spat, and jerked a thumb at Polacek, who was swelling with in-dignation that had not yet quite reached the stage of words. "Tried to change his mind," said the hunter. "This way."

The road was no more than a track down the mountain whose peak the castle occupied, a track so steep moreover that one had to walk with care, watching the skirts of one's jelab. They were already below timberline, and had to duck under the branches of tall trees along their way. A cool mountain breeze hissed through the pines and ruffled the brushes on Shea's and Polacek's turbans.

Shea unhooked the sword he had taken from Atlantès' cabinet, drew it out, and looked it over before fastening it to his outside sash. Like the one he had used in the court-yard, this sword had a rounded point and a thick, heavy blade—useless for thrusting and awkward on the parry, al-together better suited to a slashing fanatic on horseback than to a methodical épée fencer.

"Think we're gonna run into anything?" asked Polacek with wide eyes. "I ought to have something like that if we are." He turned to Echegaray and pointed to the huge broad knife in the latter's belt. "Hey, how about lending me that thing for a while? If we have any trouble it would be better to have all of us armed."

"No. Mine," said the hunter shortly, and took up the way again. Three hours brought them to the foot of the main peak. There the path began climbing and dipping across a series of spurs reaching down from another crest that thrust in from their right. The forest grew thicker here. Echegaray led them into the throat of a valley where a stream dropped past in a series of waterfalls and the tcn-a.-m. sun failed to reach the bottom. The gorge widened to a valley which held a patch of swamp, where they had to squish almost ankle-deep along the edge of a pond. Shea jumped and Polacek stopped at a glimpse of white skin and gauzy wings as the waterfays, or whatever they were, ducked out of sight. Echegaray pushed ahead without looking back and they had to follow.

Beyond, the valley narrowed again. The mountain wall closed in so sharply on their side of the stream that they had to cross on a bridge which was formed of a single log. Echegaray simply walked across as if the log had been level land. Shea followed with difficulty, waving his arms for balance, and just barely making it with a leap at the end. Polacek stuck his thumbs into his sash and tried to imitate the hunter's jaunty step, but failed to watch his footing and fell in.

"Time to eat," said the hunter as Polacek climbed out of the shallow water, rubbing his shin and cursing with a verve to curl the leaves.

Echegaray abruptly perched himself on the edge of the bridge-log, unslung his pack, and brought out a piece of bread and a slab of dried meat, each of which he expertly divided into three portions with a slash of his knife, then waved a hand at the stream. "Water," he said.

As they munched and flexed tired muscles, Polacek said: "Say, Harold, how do you know where we're going and whether we'll find Roger there—not that I want to?"

"I don't," said Shea. He turned to the hunter. "How are you sure we'll find Roger in this direction?"

"Best place," said Echegaray with mouth full.

"Yes, but where are we?" He produced a piece of parchment on which Atlantès had drawn a sketch-map when the journey was decided upon. "We've twisted around so many times in this valley that I'm not quite sure which direction the castle lies in."

"Magic?" asked Echegaray, pointing to the map.

"No. Just a map."

"What?"

"A map. You know, a picture of the country with the roads and castles and things."

"Magic," said Echegaray flatly.

"Okay, it's magic if you like it that way. Now, if you'll show us just where we are on the map—"

"We aren't," said Echegaray.

"What do you mean, we aren't? We can't have walked far enough to get off the map."

"Never on map. We're on log." He patted it to make sure.

Shea sighed. "All I want is for you to show me the spot on the map corresponding to the place where we are now."

Echegaray shook his head. "Don't understand magic."

"Oh, to hell with magic. Look at this thing. Here's Castle Carena."

"No. Castle's a long way from here. We walk fast."

"No, no! This place on the map means Castle Carena. Now we want to know where we are, on the map."

Echegaray pushed back his leather cap and scratched his short black hair. Then his brows cleared. "Want us on map?"

"Yes. You're getting the idea."

The hunter took the map from Shea's hand, turned it around a couple of times, laid it on the ground, smoothed it out, and stood up—

"Hey!" yelped Shea. He caught Echegaray's shoulders and pushed him back just as the hunter's boot was coming down on the parchment. "What's the idea of stepping on my map?"

Echegaray sat down, a resigned expression on his face. "Said you wanted us on map. Magic carpet, no?"

"No. I didn't mean you were to be on the map physically." How the devil, wondered Shea, could you explain the principles of semantics to a one-groove mind like this?"

"Whyn't you say so? First you want us on map. Then you don't. Can't make up your mind. Never saw such people."

Shea folded the map and put it back in his sash. "Let's forget it. What makes you think you're going to find Roger in this direction?"

"Best place."

"One-two-three-four-five-six-seven. Why is it the best place? What would he be doing in this direction rather than any other?"

"Crossroads. Knights always fight at crossroads." The hunter broke off a twig and whittled it to a toothpick. He used it with relish, pausing now and again to belch.

"Ready?" he said presently. Shea and Polacek nodded. Echegaray adjusted his pack, picked up his crossbow, and swung ahead.

The stream hung with them past another waterfall, where

an animal of some sort went crashing through the thicket and Echegaray with an instinctive motion whipped up his crossbow. Shea could not help thinking how Belphebe—if it were she—would be enjoying this country. Beyond, the path carried them across another high spur and through a screen of trees down to a three-pronged fork, the tracks in both directions broader and scarred by hoofmarks. Echegaray strode to the junction and looked along first one leg of the fork and then the other, his forehead contorted by thought.

"What's the matter?" said Shea. "I don't see our friend Roger here. Is that it?"

The hunter gave him a look that showed disesteem for those who wasted words pointing out the obvious, and pointed in the direction that must be south by the sun's position. "Crossroads; village. Four miles." Then he pointed north. "Crossroads. Village. Twelve miles. Which?" He looked at Shea for orders.

"Say," said Polacek. "Why don't we split up and play the field? One of us would have more chance of talking that big lug into coming back than both together, and besides I know enough magic now to take care of myself—"

"No," said Shea firmly. "You try just one more spell and I'll have your neck and ears." He turned to Echegaray. "Which way is Lord Roger most likely to go?"

The hunter shrugged. "Both. You tell."

Shea thought: after all, why not let Polacek and Echegaray take one road while he took the other? Votsy couldn't get into too much trouble with this simple-minded but knowledgeable retainer holding his hand, and as for himself, he would just as soon not have the Bounding Czech around if he should chance to meet Belphebe. The way to the north wound among trees.

"Look here," he said, "maybe that's a good idea of yours after all, Votsy. Suppose you and Echegaray take that road to the south and let me strike off on the other one. That way we'll be all right. Watch out for Belphebe, will you? She's supposed to be wandering around somewhere and I shouldn't want anyone taking pot-shots at her."

"Me neither," said Polacek. "Boy, could I use one of those cocktails she used to mix, right now! She's better than you since you taught her."

They shook hands, and Shea said: "Got any money?

Good. Might be an idea to buy yourself some kind of weapon in the village if you can. Probably a mace; anybody can swing a club without practice. Start back in about four days whether you find him or not."

"Don't worry about me," said Polacek. "I figure I know how to get along with these yaps. Look how I contacted that purple guy with the booze in the castle when all you did was sit around on your duff."

Shea turned up the road, looking back once to wave as the other two disappeared down a slope behind trees. He wondered how long Polacek's short legs would stand the pace. It was in such a wood that he had first seen the girl, light-footed, with a feather in her hat, who announced her presence with an arrow that slew the Losel. Belphebe. His feet picked the way along without any conscious help from his mind, except that he was aware of going forward. And they'd been getting so beautifully adjusted, too. . . . No, not quite such a wood either. This one was more open; the trees were smaller and there was less brush. One could see—

One could see something moving among the trunks to the right, too large and too steady of progress to be an animal. Shea snapped to attention, whipped out the sword, and slipped into the cover of a tree. The something answered his movement with a call of "Olé!" and stepped into plain view. Echegaray.

"What in the blue-belted blazes have you done with Polacek?" demanded Shea, gripping his sword firmly as the hunter trotted up.

"Left him. Talks too much. Go with you."

"Don't you know he's not fit to be allowed out without a keeper? Suppose you get right back there and keep an eye on him!"

For answer the hunter shrugged and gazed at the top of a tall tree with an elaborate lack of interest in anything else. Shea felt his temper rise, but there didn't seem to be much he could do about it, short of turning back along the road to overtake Polacek or going for Echegaray with the sword. He stuck his nose in the air and started along the path the way he had been going. Echegaray followed.

The trees began to crowd in from both sides, and from the bottom of a draw the way commenced to climb steeply. Shea found himself puffing, although he noted that the hunter in less hampering clothes was coming along like a machine. At the crest, the spur they had been climbing broadened out into a little plateau with colonnades of trees. Shea leaned against a big trunk, breathing deeply; Echegaray posted himself against another, the toothpick twirling in a corner of his mouth.

Twunk! Twunk! The tree jarred under the blows. Shea jumped—or tried to and found he couldn't. A long white-shafted arrow had pinned his sleeve to the tree, and another was affixed just beside his right leg. He caught a glimpse of Echegaray's astonished brown face as the hunter flung himself flat, then began to snake forward to the shelter of a fallen trunk, the crossbow dragging. He whipped a curved iron rod out of his boot and slipped one end of it over a stud in the side of the bow. A bolt dropped in; Echegaray's arm brought the piece of metal back and the bow was cocked.

There were no more arrows and the forest was silent. Echegaray's right hand scrubbed loose a pebble, which he tossed with a little noise into a bush at the far end of the log, at the same time peering cautiously around the near end.

"Drop!" he told Shea in a stage-whisper.

"Can't," said Shea. Thinking what a beautiful target he made for the unseen archer, he was trying to get the arrows out with his left hand. However, the position was awkward, and the deeply embedded shaft was made of some springy wood that would not break under his fingers' best efforts. His clothes were of a heavy, tweedy wool that would neither tear nor slide up the arrow. He gave a heave, then began trying to work his arm loose from the garment itself. Out of the corner of his eye he saw Echegaray watching the woods with bright-eyed attention, then bring the crossbow up slowly. . . .

Snap! The bolt flashed away among the trees with a bee-like hum. Someone laughed and Echegaray snatched up his cocking-lever.

Before he could finish reloading a voice roared: "Yield thee, sirrah! Halloo, halloo, and a mort!" Out of nowhere an oversized man had appeared over the hunter, waving a two-handed, cross-hilted sword. He was ruddy-faced, with features so strikingly regular that they might have been copied from those of an imaginary Apollo. Around his neck was a scarf with diagonal stripes of red, blue, and brown, the ends of which were tucked into a leather jacket. A light steel cap allowed curling blond hair to escape round its edges, and a huge curled horn was strapped to his back.

Echegaray rolled over twice, whipping out his knife and coming up to one knee, but the point of the big sword was right in his face and he thought better of it. He sullenly dropped his weapon and spread his hands.

Down among the trees whither the crossbow bolt had flown, a hat with a feather came into view. The hat was bobbing on the end of a stick held by a girl in a knee-length tunic, a girl with freckles and reddish-gold hair cut in a long bob. She trotted toward them as though she were going to break into a dance step at any moment, and the other hand held a longbow with an arrow already nocked.

"Belphebe!" cried Harold Shea, his heart giving a great leap.

The girl, who had been looking at Echegaray, turned toward Shea with her eyebrows up. "What said you, Saracen? I hight Belphegor."

Shea looked blank. "Don't you remember? Harold Shea. Just an old husband of yours. The picnic."

She laughed. "Nor husband nor loveling have I, and had I such, 'twould be no son of black Mahound."

"You don't know anyone named Belphebe?"

There was a flicker between her brows. Shea remembered with sinking heart what Chalmers had told him about his wife's loss of memory. She turned to the big man: "Nay, my lord Astolph, methinks this rogue doth seek to cozen us."

"Rather. This other chappie is Atlantès' hunter again, right?"

"Aye. Small tiding shall we have from him, even though he be ware of all. Recall you not when erst we caught him? Your bolts, Master Echegaray!" She held out a hand, and the hunter, muttering something about "damned women . . . spinning-wheels" thrust forward a fistful of bolts.

"So? Have we them all?" The girl pulled the bandolier toward her and snatched out another bolt. "A clever rogue, is it not?"

Echegaray shrugged. "Worth trying," he said resignedly.

"Very well, my man, you may go," said the man who had been addressed as Astolph. "And I'll trouble you to keep on your own side of the line hereafter." Echegaray picked up his crossbow and silently disappeared among the trees.

The big man turned to Shea: "Now let's have a word with

you, my fine Saracen fowl!" He stepped to the tree and wrenched out the arrows with a strength that made the task look easy. "I don't believe I've seen you before. Do you claim you know Belphegor?"

"Look here," said Shea. "I'm neither a Saracen nor a fowl, and I either married this girl or someone enough like her to be her twin sister. But she doesn't remember me."

"Daresay. It's a woman's privilege to forget, you know. They call it changing their minds, haw haw. But that's neither here nor there. We simply can't have you boffers from Carena running around and treating people the way Atlantès did this young lady. So you'd better stand and deliver an account of yourself if you want to keep that jolly head of yours."

Shea flared up. "Stand and deliver! Listen here, Dick Turpin, suppose *you* give *me*—"

"Dick Turpin? Wasn't he the highwayman chap from old England? Haw, haw, well said, oh. But I say, how would you know about him?"

"How would you?"

"We're asking the questions here, young fella. Belphegor, keep that arrow on him. Who—by Jove, don't tell me you're a wizard from my own universe, the one that's built around the British Isles?"

"I don't know how much of a wizard I'd rate, but I'm from there, all right. Only from the State of Ohio."

"American, as I live! Extrawdin'ry people, Americans—give me a million dollars or I'll cut your rug for a loop of houses, what? Isn't Ohio where the cinema colony is? Hollywood? No, that's in your province of Florida. Are you a gangster? I would say so, or you'd not be hand-in-glove with those paynims at Carena."

"I'm not a gangster and I keep telling you I'm not a Saracen. In fact if you'll step into the woods with me I'll prove it. These are only the clothes they gave me to put on," and Shea launched into a thumbnail sketch of his apportation.

"I say," said Astolph, "this chap Chalmers, your colleague, must be quite an adept. Don't know that I could do as well, though Malagigi could. Unfortunately they've laid him by the heels. Do you know my old friend Merlin?"

"You mean the famous one, the Welsh wizard? Is he still around?"

"Certainly. I meet him at the Sphinx Club in London. Do you know him?"

"I'm afraid I never met him personally."

Astolph's handsome face went a trifle grim. "That's unfortunate. Really, you know, with a war toward, we can't have strange wizards running around the borders of the Emperor Charles' dominions. Someone must vouch for you."

"There's Doc Chalmers."

"Another American. Doubtless another gangster."

"Echegaray."

"Atlantès' man. Come, you don't expect me to accept that, do you? Anything he said in your favor would be a guarantee of bad faith, assuming you could get him to say anything."

"Well, there's Lord Roger. He won't say anything in my favor."

"A fool."

"I have a friend around here somewhere, who came with me—"

"Still another gangster! Really, old man, you're only making things worse. I can't let you go under the circumstances, and I can hardly use you as a prisoner for exchange, since there's no war as yet. So there's only one thing to do . . ."

Shea, perspiring at this reasoning, cried: "Belphebe!"

There was a frown of puzzlement on the girl's face, but she shook her head. "He has the proper figure of a man, but—my lord, I know him not."

"I have the high justice," said Astolph, as though that settled everything. "Kneel down."

"Damned if I do," said Shea, tugging at his sword and reckless of Belphebe's nocked shaft.

"Righto," said Astolph, making a restraining motion at the girl. "But half a tick. Are you base-born? Most Americans are."

"I'm not a duke or anything, but I've been made a knight, if that will do. By Sir Artegall of Faerie."

"Splendid. Ordeal of battle, and sound law, too. Only right to let a chap go out on his feet. Too bad you can't be shriven."

Shea got the sword out and shucked off his Muslim coats. As soon as he came within reach, Astolph took a stance, swung the big blade up, and struck down overhand with a wood-chopper's swing. Clang! Clang! Clang! Shea parried with the awkward blade, though the force of

Astolph's stroke almost drove it from his hand. He took a backhand cut with it, which Astolph parried easily, then came back forehand, but his opponent jumped away with a lightness surprising in so big a man. His return was so rapid that he forced Shea to give ground.

The duke was good but not too good. After the third exchange Shea felt he could parry anything the big blade sent at him. However, the next clash brought a trickle of worry. Astolph's reach and length of blade were keeping him too far away for this clumsy weapon to be used as it was supposed to be used. If he could parry, he could not cut home, and in time the big man would wear him down.

Another whirl and he almost lost his sword. The handle was slippery in his grasp. He began to grow angry at the unfairness of this big lug, and with difficulty remembered that an angry fencer is a losing one.

Astolph drove him back again, almost into a tree, and lowered his blade for a second to get a better purchase. The sight of the exposed chest brought Shea's fencing reflexes to the surface. His right arm shot out, with the whole weight of his body behind it in a long lunge. The rounded point of the sword hit jacket and chest with a thump. Astolph, a little off balance and not expecting such a push, sat down.

"Yield thee yourself!" shouted Shea, standing over him and sighting on the Englishman's neck.

The duke's left arm came around like a jibing main boom and swept Shea's ankles from under him. Down went Shea. He was struggling in a bone-crushing wrestler's grip when he heard the girl cry: "Hold, enough! By the power of woods and water which is my domain, I bid you cease!"

She felt Astolph relax unwillingly and climbed to his own feet. A rill of blood trickled from the duke's nose where Shea had butted him, while Shea's turban was in his eyes, one of which was swelling, and the other end of the head-dress was draped around him like one of Laocoön's serpents.

"I say, my dear," said Astolph, "you can't do this, you know. Ordeal of battle goes to a finish, and anything left of the loser has to be burned. I shall complain to the Emperor." He bent over, reaching for the big sword.

"Halt, sir! Would you try my bodkin?" She had drawn the tough shaft to the head and it pointed steadily at the big man's midriff. "I care not for the Emperor Charles of the Lord of Circassia in this domain. But I say this is a true man that has fought well, and that spared you when he might have slain, and be he Saracen or no, there shall henceforth be peace between you."

Astolph grinned and held out his hand to take Shea's in a hearty grip. "Needs must take the fortune of war. Jolly good thing you didn't make that hit with a pointed blade or I should have been properly skewered. I daresay you can show me a trick or two. Care to join forces?"

"I'm not sure," said Shea. "What kind of campaign do you have on?" He thought: if I can only get her to Chalmers, he can bring back her memory. In the meantime not all of Atlantès' ifrits will pry me away from her.

"This bloody—excuse me, old girl—this Castle of Carena. Atlantès has Lord Roger in there, and there's a prophecy that our side can't win the war unless we convert him."

Shea snickered. "From what I've seen of that guy, I'd say you'd have a rough time converting him to anything he didn't want to do. He hasn't got enough mind to convert with."

Astolph waved a hand. "That's all right. He saw Brada-mant, the lady warrior, you know, at the Fountain of Love, and fell in love with her when he drank from it, so he can't do anything but what she wishes, at least until the spell is taken off. Atlantès was going to fly him to the Fountain of Forgetfulness, but I've bagged the mount."

A wave of relief swept over Shea. "You mean Brada-mant is the lady warrior who is supposed to steal Roger from the Saracens? I was afraid—" and he gave a quick résumé of Chalmers' position with Florimel at Castle Carena, and why he had come hunting the big beef.

When he had finished, Belphebe said: "My lord duke, said I not it was a proper man? Sir, I thank you for your gentleness toward me; you may make me your devoirs." She whipped a knife like a steel sliver from her own belt and, taking down her cap, daintily split the feather in it along the middle, and handed Shea one half. "My favor."

Feeling awkward and a trifle confused, he tried to fix it in his breast. Silly, starting one of those formalized medieval courtships with its gambits and counters at this stage in their relationships . . .

Said Astolph: "So Roger's on the scram, as you fellas say? Very interesting; should have told me sooner. Stupid ass, Roger, though an awfully good fighter." He paused. "Do you know, this won't quite do, my friend. You and I are rivals in a sense. We both want Shaykh Roger, and for that matter so does the Lady Bradamant, though I really can't understand why. But I'll make you an armistice, matter to be decided by dicing, or whatever you say, but no magic. Are you genuinely a wizard, by the way?"

Shea looked down. "Not a very good one, I'm afraid."

"Come, young fella; no false modesty. Just cast me a little spell and demonstrate, so that we can have confidence in each other. Nothing like confidence, you know."

"Or leather either," said Shea. "It lasts." Belphegor-Belphebe was looking at him expectantly, and for his life he could not recall the passes of the somatic element that seemed so important in the magic of this space-time continuum. Wait a minute, though—there was the little spell Chalmers had used the other day to demonstrate that very point. The passes were simple and made a plant grow before the eyes; in Doc's case, a snapdragon. Grass would do to start with; it ought to make some kind of important-looking plant. Shea plucked a handful, laid it on the ground and knelt over it, closing his eyes in the effort of memory as he whispered:

> "Though sore be my sowing,
>   And more than ye know,
> And the end of my growing
>   Is only to grow;
> Yet I cease not of growing for lightnings above
>   me or death-worms below."

When he looked around again there was no sign of a plant. Nor any of the grass. He wondered what he had done wrong this time.

Astolph was looking straight at him. "By Jove! That's a neat bit, Sir Harold. Quite as good as Malagigi could have done. Apologies, old man."

"What is?" asked Shea. His voice sounded strangely muffled as though he were speaking through a blanket. Which, as he learned by putting his hand to his face, just what he was doing. His beard, sprouting at about an inch a second, had already spread down his chest and across his shoulders, the ends twisting and curling like the tips of thin and inquisitive worms. The beard passed his belt-line and engulfed his arms.

Frantically he tried to think of a counter-spell, and felt as though he were in Hell when the only thing he could remember was Chalmers' all-too-effective spell for raising dragons. Live dragons growing out of one's face, ugh! Or would it be snakes? The beard had passed his knees, his ankles, its questing points had reached the ground. Belphegor stared at him open-mouthed.

"Oh, bravo!" said Astolph.

The stuff was piling up on the ground in a little haycock. If it would only lay off a minute; give him a respite to think! He wondered desperately how long it would keep going if he failed to find the counter-spell. There was the mill that had ground the ocean full of salt. That might be legend, but in a universe where magic worked there was apparently nothing to stop such a process until coils of hair filled the forest and rose like a tide round the magic flames that now encircled the Castle of Carena. He stepped back, almost tripping over a root. If that pulsating hair got him down—But wait, maybe he could get Astolph to stop it. If the duke claimed Merlin as an acquaintance, he ought to know something of magic.

"Had enough?" he called over the growing mattress of wool to Astolph, whose head was now just visible.

"Thanks, yes."

"All right, fair's fair. Let's see you take the spell off."

"Righto." Astolph shifted his big sword to his left hand and swung it through the air, making a few expert passes with his right and mumbling a spell. The young mountain of first-rate upholstering-material vanished, and Shea tenderly felt his smooth cheeks. "You must meet Merlin some day," said the Duke. "Nobody likes a good joke like old Merlin. But I say, shall we get on with the business? Do you know, I believe the whole problem would become rather simple if we could get your friend out of Carena."

"I'm not sure he wants to get out," said Shea. "There's the question of Florimel."

"No trouble at all, old man. With a pair like you and your principal, we ought to be able to rescue Malagigi from Albracca, and it would be jolly odd if he couldn't do something for the lady. But I really don't see—" he went off into frowning concentration.

"What?" asked Shea.

"That wall of flame. Deuced awkward. That is, I know well enough how to deal with it, only we can't apply the solution."

"Sir Harold has been made immune to it," said Belphegor.

"Ah, but the problem is not smuggling him in, but getting this Lady—ah—Florimel out. It's this way, you see—" the big man turned to Shea with a wide gesture. "The Lady Bradamant owns a magical ring, very superior production, which protects one from any sort of enchantments, and also makes one invisible if taken into the mouth. It would be just the thing for your Florimel. Bradamant intended to use it to break into Carena for Roger, but she loaned it to Roland for no reason, and the silly beggar accidentally drank at the Fountain of Forgetfulness and lost his wits. Completely blotto. Can't remember where he put the ring or that there is a ring; can't even remember his name."

"I think I see," said Shea. "If we can get Roland to remember where the ring is, then one of us can extract Florimel from Carena and start all over again. But who's Roland? Is he important?"

"Really, old man! One of the twelve. The paladins. The companions of Emperor Charles. Best man of the lot in a fight."

"Oh," said Shea. The thought had occurred to him that this was not a problem in magic at all. Roland sounded like a fairly simple case of amnesia, and there was no reason why the techniques of the Garaden Institute should not work quite as well among these mountains as in Ohio. "I think I know a spell that will restore Roland's wits," he said. And if Roland's, he thought, why not Belphebe's? He must watch for a chance to try.

"Really? That would be wonderful. What do you say we go about it? Buttercup must be about somewhere." He put his forefingers in his mouth and whistled piercingly.

Something moved in the forest and a hippogriff trotted into view, wings folded neatly back against its flanks. The wings were mainly white with pulsations of rainbow hues flickering through them. The animal pricked up its ears as it came and poked at Astolph with its beak. He scratched among the roots of its feathers. "It answers me better than it ever did Atlantès," he said. "Those confounded Saracens don't know how to treat animals."

"What does it eat?" asked Shea practically. "I don't see how that eagle's head goes with a horse's digestive apparatus."

"Blooms from some of those African plants, I believe. Buttercup's not a heavy eater. Very well, everybody, all aboard! Bit crowded, what? What's that remark you Americans make when punching cattle? Brutal business that, by the bye; I never could see why you don't just herd the poor things instead of punching them. Oh, yes, yippee. *Yippee!*"

CHAPTER 8

THE HIPPOGRIFF TROTTED SWAYINGLY UP A rise. Shea imagined that it would not be very fast on the ground, thanks to the interference between the magnified claws on the forefeet and the hooves behind. As they reached the granite hogback of the crest, the claws clung securely enough to the rock, but the hooves skidded alarmingly. Shea clutched Belphebe-Belphegor around the midriff, and she clutched Astolph, who did not seem at all perturbed. The hippogriff spread its wings, blundered along the ridge, flapping furiously, slipped again, teetered over a fifty-foot drop, leaped into the air, swept down and then up in a smooth curve that just missed the treetops.

"Whew!" said Shea, the wind of the heights on his face and a jelly-like feeling in his center. "Sir Astolph, I think your Buttercup should use a rocket-assisted take-off."

"Wouldn't do, old man," said Astolph, over his shoulder. "Laws of nature diff . . . frame of reference . . ." His words whirred away down the wind of their passage as Shea reflected that according to the theory of dynamics, this beast wouldn't even be able to get off the ground. The contact with Belphebe sent tingles up his arms; he wanted to get her away for a good long talk. She seemed unaware of the emotion she was provoking.

The hippogriff apparently disliked the weight of its triple load and at every landing it sighted below, tried to spiral in for a landing. Astolph had to bark to keep it on course. After the third of these aborted efforts, Shea saw a cleared area of some extent; the details grew slowly to those of a small village with thatched roofs, surrounded by a patchwork of planted fields, plowed ground and weedy meadow. The hippogriff, its horse end sweating, swooped eagerly down, skimmed the ground, pulled into a stall, and made a four-point landing that jarred Shea's teeth.

71

He climbed down and reached up a hand to help Belphebe, but she vaulted down without seeing him and he felt foolish. With the half-unconscious effort one makes to cover embarrassments, he swung toward the cottages, and as he did so, a chorus of screams burst from them. Men and women boiled out of one after another, running for their lives. They were either deeply or suspiciously sunburned, and most wore nothing but long, dirty, ragged shirts, and the speed of their passage took no notice of hippogriff or riders.

After the spreading rout came two men. The shorter of the pair, a good-looking, youngish fellow with strong hands, seemed to be trying to pacify the other. The second individual wore the medieval-type garments with hosen and turn-up shoes Shea had seen in Faerie, but with the laces of his jacket dangling. His face was unbarbered and his eyes roved. The fists waved in jerky motions; the voice growled.

"Upon my soul!" said Astolph. "Look here, you chaps, cheerio, and all that."

The shorter man gave a glance, waved a momentary hand, clamped a wrist-lock on the other and led him over to the newcomers. Shea perceived that the wild man would be handsome in a Latin sort of way if cleaned up.

"Greetings, most noble Astolph," said the short man, with as near an approach to a bow as he could manage with his grip on the other, "and to you, fair Belphegor, hail. The wrath is on our great companion once more; he had slain half the village, had I not let him. Yet in true gentilesse, the fault be not wholly his own."

"Indeed? Tell us about it, old man," said Astolph.

"Would you believe it, fair lady, and you, gentles? A hart of eight brought I home, as pricksome a bit of venison as ever a man saw before vespers. A meal for the Emperor's own majesty, one might think; make it a pie, or what will you? Nay, these base varlets must even serve it up boiled, as though 'twere salt stockfish in Lent. I gagged, but our friend Roland put down the first two bites fairly enough. At the third, meseems he must have recovered a whit of the laws of cookery, for he gave a great howl like a lion and set upon the knaves, beating in their heads with his fists. But alas, to what purpose? Not even a crack will let savor into such skulls."

He looked round the group and his eye came to rest on

Shea. "A Paynim, ha! I thank you, Lord Astolph; a cut from his haunch will recompense me my venison." He gave a barking laugh to demonstrate that this was meant for humor. Shea smiled dutifully.

"Ah—er—" said Astolph. "Lord Reinald of Montalban, may I present to you Sir Harold de Shea? A johnny from England—that is, from one of our subject allies." He swung to Shea. "I'd be glad to present you to Count Roland d'Anglante, except that as you see, the poor lad wouldn't recognize you." The Count, who was apparently the wild man, was alternately sucking one finger and tapping the end of it in the palm of the hand on which Lord Reinald retained his grip. It seemed to provide him with deep satisfaction. "Sir Harold is also looking for Roger of Carena. Small world, isn't it?"

"The chase is like to be longer than that for Angelica," said Reinald, reaching his free hand inside his jacket and producing something which Shea did not quite make out to kiss before he went on. "We have it on the word of the kerns that Sir Roger passed through at spark of dawn, moving as though Saint Beelzebub were on his slot."

"Really, old man!" cried Astolph. "I must be losing my grip; to hear that he slipped past my watch is more startling than your canonization of Beelzebub."

Reinald shrugged and resisted a sudden jerk by his companion. "Let buy a candle for Lucifer, then. The thing's established—would you doubt my word?"

"No, but—look, here, old man, it's rather important for the Emperor. Whyn't you stop him?"

"Can a man live forever like a priest? Roland slept; I tied him to a rafter and sought a damsel who had made certain signs by the fountain."

"How perfectly rotten of you!" cried Astolph. "What the devil did you funk the job for?"

Reinald grimaced. "Angelica lost, and fair Belphegor drives me to a distance with arrows sharper than Saint Cupid's own. What's left of life?"

There seemed not much more to say. They walked back toward the village, Astolph fingering his chin. He looked up to remark: "Do you know, I believe Sir Roger will head west, then double back to join Agramant's army. Sort of thing he would consider the height of cleverness." He turned to Shea.

"Your gangster friend with the odd name won't find him. That direction would be the double bluff."

He paused and, pulling the hippogriff's head down to his lips, said something in its ear that sounded like a series of low-toned whistles. The animal cocked an intelligent eye at him and stood still.

Among the huts a table stood under a tree, and on it lay two large wooden plates heaped with boiled meat which gave off a powerful odor of garlic and was framed in congealing grease. There were no other plates in sight, nor anything to drink.

While the others waited politely Reinald went from door to door, shouting in each without result, then returned, shaking his head gloomily. "The rats have fled the larder," he said. "Beyond the mind of reasonable man to riddle out. Sir Harold, how wags it in your country? Would not men without number be glad and overglad to have lords of Charles' own court to hold them from harm?"

Shea raised his eyebrows. "It couldn't be that they're afraid of your friend's tempers?"

"Think you so, indeed?" Reinald's eye brightened and he nodded his head as though something new and important had come into his life. "They be base-born enough. Three or four has he slain, but no more; and even those without pretension to gentle blood. It might be, though; fear of death is ever dreadful to those who know it not for a mocker. A mystery."

The five made room on a couple of rough-hewn benches and divided the meat with knives supplied by Reinald and Astolph, washing it down with water from the village well, drunk from the bucket. Shea hoped that the fauna of this continuum did not include typhoid germs, the back of his mind assuring him comfortingly that the deadliest disease present would probably be African fever induced by night air. All the same when he noticed a crawfish clinging to the moss inside the bucket, he and the crawfish pointedly ignored each other.

Reinald gnashed his teeth across a bone and addressed Astolph: "Start we tonight or attend the Lady Bradamant, the mirror of true valor?"

Said Astolph: "I don't really believe we gain anything by a night march, do you? After all, it will be hard going with Count Roland in such a state, and we won't really lose anything, since I doubt if Roger is up to a night march. Up with the birds, then . . . but wait a tick. Our young friend here is a jolly good qualified magician, and says he knows a spell to bring Roland's wits back."

Reinald crossed himself. "Holy Saint Virgil, protect us! Those wits lost to black Mahound!"

"Would simplify—"

Count Roland, who had been slobbering over his meat, suddenly turned round to look at Shea and said in a loud, clear voice: "You Saracen! I slay you!" and leaped from his place, trotting around the table with dirty hands outstretched.

"Get him—" yelled Astolph, as the others scrambled to their feet, but the latter was upon Shea before he could more than get on his feet. He did the only thing he could think of at the moment to save his neck without bringing the others down upon him; viz, ducked, knocked the clutching right hand up with his own left and dug his own right with all his strength into the Count's belly. It was like punching a truck-tire, but Roland staggered two steps, almost upset the table, sat down with a fish-like expression, spreading across his face, and as he recovered his breath, began to cry.

Shea, shaking his hand to get the tingle out of his knuckles, almost laughed at the sight of Reinald's open mouth. "By my halidome!" said the Paladin. "A rude stroke was that."

"Oh, yes," said Astolph. "Quite good at the thrust, this young fella; nearly gutted me like a bird a bit back. If you ever fight him, Lord Reinald, guard against that straight lunge. Now look here, I think we can reach an agreement. Sir Harold, I take it, only wants Roger to exchange him for a brace of friends, now in durance in Castle Carena, where that blighter Atlantès is holding them in chancery. If he can restore Roland's wits for us, I say that with three Paladins, we ought to be able to set him on the right track."

Reinald blinked once or twice in a way Shea found not altogether pleasing. "The Lady Bradamant would stand our certain aid, I doubt not," he said. "Is aught of philosophical apparatus required for your enchantment, Sir Harold?"

"No-o-o. Not that I know of; unless you have a night-light."

"That wot I not of; but since there be no bar and our composition waits but on your action, speed on. It is good law that the vavassour render his service before he have his sustention."

Shea looked at Belphegor (whom he insisted upon calling Belphebe in his mind), but she was looking in the other direction, after a single glance. He was not at all sure that he understood what Reinald was saying and he would much rather have a tête-à-tête with his wife, but as near as he could make out, the two Paladins were making a deal with him to get Doc and Florimel out of Castle Carena if he got Count Roland out of what seemed to be a case of simple throwback amnesia. He sighed and addressed himself to the task by turning toward the still softly sniffling Paladin:

"There, there, that didn't really hurt much, did it? But when little boys are bad, they have to learn . . ." Belphegor's mouth fell open a little as he droned on, but the wild man looked at Shea interestedly, then suddenly seized him around the neck and implanted a greasy kiss on his cheek.

Reinald laughed openly; Astolph seemed to have some difficulty in controlling his breath for a moment and announced that he was for bed. Shea turned toward the pale blue eyes now fixed on his in adoration.

"Want a story?" he asked. "If you'll come along I'll tell you one about three—dragons." The pattern seemed simple; age was suppressed beyond about a three-year-old level. He said rapidly over his shoulder to the others: "This is going to take some time, if the spell will work at all. You-all will have to get away from here and wait a while. I could use insulin shock, but that piece of philosophical apparatus isn't around, so I'll probably have to work half the night by my own method."

They went, willingly enough and yawning under the declining light. Roland listened with interest to the story of the three bears, translated into dragons, and demanded more. "No," said Shea. "You tell me a story instead, 'cause it's way past my bedtime. Then I'll tell you one."

Roland laughed delightedly. "They're all silly go-to-bed-earlies. What 'tory you want?"

"Well, tell me who you are."

"I'm me."

"Sure. You live in a cave, don't you?" Bits of the *Orlando Furioso* were floating through Shea's head; or was it the *Chanson de Roland?* He wished he could get them straight, but seemed to be doing all right so far, since his patient remained attentive. "And your mother's name is Madame Bertha. But what does she call you?"

"Gay-gay. That means 'snookums,' an' it's white and red."

Shea grunted internally. This mass of muscle, hair and dirt was about as far from a snookums as he could conceive; but at least the white and red was a tiny advance; those were Roland's colors. That was in the book. "What else do they call you?"

"Ruffy."

Not much there. "What's your father like?"

A pout. "Don't know. Gone to fight Saxons."

"Didn't he come back?"

The heavy face became woebegone. "Don't know."

"Yes, you do. No tell, no story."

Roland began to sniffle a little and Shea did not altogether blame him. It must have been pretty rough to move out of a castle into a cave where you didn't get enough to eat. But he was inexorable; Roland finally stopped sniffling and remarked: "Mama said he gained glory, and the syndics said we mustn' live there any more, and I was cold and had a fight and saw a fat man sitting in an inn and somebody blew a music and I don't like it here and I'm hungry."

The ice was beginning to crack. Shea felt a jump of joy in his heart and looked around for Belphegor, but she had vanished. With elaborately affected scorn, he said: "I know a better story than that."

"You do not, either! The fat man was a crownèd king, and he was my mama's brother . . ."

A solemn moon came up and winked through the leaves, then settled slowly toward disappearance-point again as Shea desperately flogged his own memory and the Paladin's on the details of the vanished career. Once he thought he was going to lose his man, when Roland mentioned the name of Angelica, put down his head and wept for quite five minutes; once he thought all would come clear at once, when Shea threw in the name of the giant Ferragus, and the Paladin seized a bone from the table, leaping up and shouting "Montjoie!" But that one only collapsed into babbling, and it must have been well past midnight, a poor hour for this country, when Roland once more got to his feet, and pressed the heels of both palms to his eyes.

"Sir," he said, "I know not your name aright nor true condition, and I am hindered from giving you the kiss of peace, since I perceive my own condition is less than that which knight and gentleman should hold. You have my favor; are you a necromancer?"

"I suppose I know something about magic," said Shea, suddenly feeling modest.

"I trust your penance will be small. There be others of our brotherhood about, an I mistake not?" He looked toward where the moon was losing its struggle. "Let us seek them; I see it all, we must seek mount and away for time will press. Is the Lady Bradamant among them?"

CHAPTER 9

THE LADY BRADAMANT WAS NOT IN THE HEAD-
man's house where Duke Astolph and Reinald were laid out
with straw in their ears, the latter on his back and snoring
like a Diesel engine. What was more important for Shea,
neither was the Lady Belphegor. He felt deflated, but Count
Roland was quite evidently not of the same mind.

"Ho!" cried that worthy Paladin, in a voice that would
have made the window-panes shake if there had been any
window-panes. "Will you lie slugabed when there are deeds
to do? Rouse out, I say!"

In the dimness of the hut, Shea saw Astolph roll over,
swinging his arms. Reinald's snores checked for one moment,
then began again in a higher key.

"Ha, rouse!" Roland shouted again, and somewhat unexpectedly, deposited a resounding kick on the recumbent
form as Astolph came up, all standing. Reinald whipped up,
light as a cat, one hand to his belt, and Shea caught a
gleam of steel, but Roland laughed and extended both arms:
"Nay, nay, my noble lord and brave friend, will you slit
my weazand while still the Paynim danger lies on France?"

Reinald relaxed with a growl. Astolph threw a branch on
the dying fire, and as it blazed up, looked keenly into
Roland's face. "I believe he's all right again," he remarked.

"Aye, my own man; grace to this young knight." Roland
swung toward Shea. "Sir Harold, were I not sworn to poverty,
the treasures of Babylon would be too small for your reward. Yet know that you have all my heart and true support
in whatsoever shall not run counter to my knightly vow of
fealty to the Emperor Charles. I have the ring. And now
gentles, we must out and away." He cocked his head on one
side. "Hark, I hear the shrill trumpet!"

"Then the trumpeter will have outwatched the bear," said
Reinald, dryly. "Look you, good Roland, this quest of Roger

gains naught by a night-march while we have Astolph, who can ride after him by day on the wings of the wind. Take then your rest; with the dawn we'll woo fortune."

"He's quite right, you know," said the Duke through a yawn. "Besides, I daresay you could do with a bath and some weapons before undertaking anything serious, and to-night there's precious little chance of your getting—"

He stopped, looking over Shea's shoulder, and the latter turned with a jump of the heart to see standing in the low doorway—Belphegor, arrow on string and the firelight throwing lovely shadows on her face.

She came a couple of paces into the room. "I heard the bruit, my lords, and thought—"

Said Reinald: "That there was something toward which might permit that after all you should take comfort in my arms?"

"Nay, my lord, I sleep lonely this night—and every other, where you're involved." She returned her arrow to its quiver and relaxed the string.

"Hey!" said Shea. "I want to see you." If that antiquated technique could work such wonders on Roland, there was better than a good chance that—

The girl inclined her head gravely. "Sir knight, you have made me your service. You may see me to my rest."

"Where is it?" he asked, as they reached the door.

"I have made my bed in the branches of an oak that overlooks these cots," she said. "My lonely bed."

Shea smiled a narrow little smile. "Mean to say you positively, positively don't remember being my wife?" and thinking that at best he'd probably have to break her of claustrophobia all over again. Being married to a girl who wouldn't sleep in a bed, he had found, was an experience that did not grow on one with repetition.

She drew away from him a little. "Now, sirrah, seek you to cozen me again? Certes, you'd be a more adroit seducer than yonder lord of Montalban, but I'll not be seduced."

Shea grinned. "I should hope not by that big lug, anyway. But say, don't you remember things?"

"Nay—that water of Forgetfulness whereof he drank have I never seen. I am free of the forests . . . and yet, and yet—there is a passage. I know not how I came to Castle Carena, save that I stood within beside a grey-haired wizard whom they called Sir Reed and his fair bride—ah, faugh!" She made a gesture of disgust.

"What's the matter with Sir Reed?"

"Not he, but that great loutish booby of a Roger. It had been insupportable but for the visit of Lord Dardinell and his squire Medoro."

"Huh?" said Shea in alarm. "What about this Medoro?"

"A most sweet lad. He took my part when all the others would have trapped me like a hare. Could I but count that he'd be more true to me than to a religion that bids him keep four wives—"

"My God, you can't do that!" cried Shea. "That's bigamy! Maybe I'd better—"

"Sir, you lose my favor when you still hold to the old tune like a musician who has only one note."

"Oh, all right, all right. Honest, darling, I'm only trying—well, skip it. How did you get out?"

"How—? Oh, one of the men there leaned on a staff, so I borrowed it from him, clouted a couple of pates, and it was ho!—and away."

"Didn't they chase you?"

"Marry, that they did, but I am somewhat lightfoot." (Shea could believe that. Looking at her hungrily as she paused under the big oak, he could remember her in a red bathing-suit, easily outdistancing himself and a squad of friends along the beach of Lake Erie.)

"Okay. Now to go back a little. You don't remember meeting Reed Chalmers and me in Faerie by shooting a Losel that was after us? And you don't remember joining us in the campaign against the Enchanters' Chapter? Or that fight in the air with Busyrane on his dragon?"

"No. Should I? These names have a barbarous, outlandish sound to me."

"You certainly should remember, and you should remember some other things, too," he said, grimly. "I think I can—"

"Put a spell upon me to work me to your will? Nay, I will assuredly contempt you from my grace, though I bade you accompany me that I might do you service."

"I'm sorry. Honest." (Shea wondered whether he ought to get down on one knee and kiss her hand, but decided he'd be damned first.)

She reached out one hand and touched his arm. "So.

Well, the service is yours in any case—not for the pretty apology, but because we of the woods love not injustice."

"What injustice?"

"Think you you have a true composition with these lords? Then think again. Duke Astolph may be moderate well affected toward you, but not Lord Reinald, who holds it lawful to deceive and despoil all Saracens, among which he'd place yourself and all your friends."

Shea grinned. "I imagined they might be trying to clear out. But I'll be watching."

"Small service will that be. Astolph is to cast a spell of deep sleep on you tonight and they depart at dawn. He offered to take me and make me his leman, but I'd have none of him."

"The—excuse me for what I'm thinking. I thought Astolph was on the square."

"Oh, aye; a good wight, surely. But wrapped in law, like all the English, and when Lord Reinald spoke of his liege duty to the Emperor, and how with Roger beyond the castle, the victory of Christendom would be delayed by contention with you for his body,—why then, Duke Astolph let himself be overborne."

Shea mused. "Will Roland let them get away with it? He seemed grateful enough when I saw him, and he certainly owes me a favor."

Belphegor laughed tinklingly. "I give him not a fig's weight—oh, a most accomplished gentle knight that will swoon devotion like a rose, but will set duty to the Emperor and his war above all else, even more than Duke Astolph. Has he found the Lady Bradamant's ring?"

"He said so."

"Then even more. For look you, this Castle Carena is a haunt of paynim sorcery and nest of vipers, which being entered by the power of the ring, Roland would destroy and hold it for the day's best deed."

It was probably true. Shea remembered that the Count had made a reservation in favor of the Emperor in his promise of gratitude. "I guess I'm stuck with finding Roger on my own, then," he said, a little sadly. "What are you going to do?"

"I? In sooth, live my free life of the woods and fountains, sobeit Medoro . . . Since Roger's free of the castle, I hold myself free of my promise to help Duke Astolph hale him forth."

"Why not help me find Roger then?"

"Wherefore should I?"

Shea felt his throat dry up. "Oh, to help beat injustice, or just for the fun of the adventure . . . or something." He finished lamely, then went on again. "After all, you did promise to help Astolph."

"Ah, sir, but a debt lay there. It was Astolph and none other who turned the pursuit from Castle Carena when they would have taken me with horse and hound."

"What! You didn't tell me that." Shea felt a homicidal impulse toward Sir Reed Chalmers, who hadn't told him, either. Sir Reed evidently felt that he'd put his foot into it about as far as he cared to.

"Aye; slew one of the Saracens and scattered the rest. But come, sir, you impose sleepless hours upon me to no purpose. You must find me an acuter reason if I am to join your search for this Roger."

"Well—he'll head for the Saracen camp to get into the war, won't he? You might find—Medoro—there."

"Oh, fie, Sir Harold! Would you have me pursue a man like that great, buxom warrior-wench, the Lady Bradamant? You think but ill of those to whom you pay your devoirs. . . . Not that you are wrong as to the fact; poet though he be, Medoro will hardly neglect the summons of the trumpet at such an hour. Nay, your reason is against companioning with you for a search in that quarter. Now I must have a new one, doubly strong."

So, the dope's a poet, is he? thought Shea. "I don't know any more reasons," he said stoutly, "Except that just I want you to come along because I love you."

Belphegor-Belphebe caught her breath for one second, then extended her hand. "So you have found the key at last, and are my true knight. It is convenanted. I give you rendezvous at this spot, so soon as the Paladins be again in slumber. Now go, ere stark suspicion o'er-spread their minds."

"What shall we do? Steal their horses?"

"Nay, the hippogriff? And Roland's steed is the great Bayard, who'd rouse his master on the instant."

"Oh, damn. I know a man named Bayard, but he'll never wake anybody up. What else—?"

"Go, sir, I said. Nay, no embraces."

"Good-night," said Shea, and made for the hut, feeling a

tremulous half-hope such as he had not known since they
were both prisoners of the Da Derga in Faerie.

He found the three squatting around the small fire on a
hearth in the center of the floor. A hole in the ceiling above
let out about a third of the smoke.

Astolph stretched, yawned, and with the air of a man pre-
paring for a long sleep, began carefully unwinding his red-
blue-brown scarf. Catching Shea's eye fixed on him, he
remarked "School" briefly, then: "One can't exactly wear a
tie in this country, you know. I had the colors made into a
scarf instead."

"What school is it for?"

"Winchester," said the Duke, with just the right note of
pride. "Oldest of 'em all, you know. Merlin's on the board
of trustees. Wonderful thing, the public-school system, though
I don't know what will become of it with all this socialism."

"I went to a public school in Cleveland myself."

"I daresay." Astolph regarded him with an air rendolent
of mistrust, and Shea perceived he had not taken the right
way to influencing people. Before he could smooth matters
out, Reinald lifted his head from where he was already
down in the straw again: "Peace, you twain! A pox on your
babble that keeps honest men from their rest."

"Righto. But first I fancy I'd better make certain Sir
Harold here doesn't wipe us in the eye. Oh, you're a man of
honor and a jolly good fellow, but this is merely a sensible
precaution." Astolph had reached his feet as lightly as a cat
while speaking and picked up the big sword, which he now
pointed at Shea. "Lie quietly, old thing and take your
medicine."

"You lie on a blanket of cloud, soft and white,
And you sleep, sleep, sleep through the murmuring
      night,
Your limbs are so heavy, your eyelids must close,
You're torpid, you're drowsy; you loll, drift and doze—"

Shea, fully aware that this was a sleeping-spell, fought to
keep his mind alert while casting about for a counter-spell.
There was the one with the paper . . . no, that was a weakness spell . . . no . . . his thoughts were losing coherency.

"Come, ye spirits who generate pandiculation
And your brothers who revel in wide oscitation—"

The spell corresponded to something like hypnotism, and it was hard to keep his eyes from the tips of Astolph's fingers, moving in the passes. It was almost not worth the trouble of trying to beat it. After all . . .

"Come Morpheus hither, and Somnus and Coma—"

There was a story where you mustn't sleep. *King of the Golden River?* No . . . *Kim*—and the boy there had used the multiplication table. The memory jerked him to effort. Three times three is nine . . . if he could only keep on . . . this part was too easy . . . six times seven is forty-two, six times eight . . . The spell droned on, apparently without end . . . eleven times thirteen is one hundred forty-three . . .

"I by this authority conjure you, sleep!"

It was over. Shea lay with his eyes closed, but his brain wide open, working on seven times fourteen. Reinald's voice came drowsily, as though the Paladin were talking through fur: "Will he sleep till the morrow?"

"Through several morrows, I should say," said Astolph. "I gave him a jolly good dose."

"Almost put me to sleep myself," said Reinald. He rolled over once, and in less than a minute was back in the low-register snore that had preceded Roland's kick.

Shea waited, wishing his nose would stop itching, or that Astolph would quiet down next to him, so he could scratch without being caught at it. His eyebrow began to itch, too, then the rest of his face in patches, so agonizingly that he wriggled it, trying to throw off the feeling. Astolph turned over and Shea froze into immobility, wondering whether a snore would be convincing, decided against it and discovered that the itch had shifted to a point inside his left ear. The Duke made another turn, loosed a sigh of comfort and seemed to drift off. But it was a good ten minutes— every one of which Shea counted—before he dared to let his eyelids flicker open.

There was a small red glow at the center of the room and an oblong of gray that was the door. Beyond, he judged it would be near the hour of false dawn; the moon had long since disappeared. The three figures in the draw made darker blacks in the blackness of the hut, but lay perfectly still, and under the beat of Reinald's snores the rythmic breathing of the other two was audible. Asleep all right, but he could not afford to take chances, therefore gave it another good ten minutes before stirring an experimental arm. The dark gray patch of the door turned abruptly bright blue, then dark gray again. Far away, thunder purred softly.

Shea thought a few unpleasant things about his luck and the weather. If the storm came this way, it would rain through that hole in the roof, certainly rousing Astolph and probably Roland. If he were to make a getaway, it would have to be right now.

He moved his hands slowly in the straw beside him, gathering up his turban, which had been serving as a pillow, and his sword. At the next rumble, he rolled to his feet, took two cautious steps and lifted his flowing outer garments from the peg where they had hung. The next two steps took him out.

A flash showed a huge pile of thunderheads nearby, and the sound came long-continued, rolling closer. A little puff of wind whirled down the village street. The hippogriff was huddled where Astolph had left it, squatted head down and eyes closed. It trembled unhappily in the lightning-flashes, its feather stirring in the vagrant dashes of wind. When Shea touched it, the beast, bound by the Duke's magic, did not lift its head. To loose the spell on it would take fooling around, time, and maybe more skill than he had. The first drop struck his hand.

A brilliant flash and an avalanche of thunder. Shea, thinking he had heard a shout from the direction of the headman's house, whipped the jelab around him and ran just as the rain came pattering down, heading without equivocation along the street and toward Belphebe's tree. As he reached the edge of the forest-shade, she stepped out before him, as wide-awake as an owl, unperturbed by the rushing rain.

"Did they—" she said; a crash of thunder drowned the rest.

"I think the storm woke them up," said Shea, shedding his outer cloak and hanging it around her. "How are we going to get out of here?"

"You an enchanter and know not this?" She laughed gaily,

turned and whistled a low, lilting tune in a minor key, less than a third audible under the pattering leaves and whipping branches.

Shea strained his eyes toward the village and in the repeated lightning-glare, was sure he saw figures moving: "Hurry," he said. Then he heard a trampling behind and a voice shouted "Whee-he-he-he! Who calls?" Almost instantly it was answered by another and higher one: "Who calls?"

"Bel—Belphegor of the woods—a daughter of—" her voice seemed to check oddly.

"In whose name call you us?" bellowed the first voice.

"In the name of Sylvanus, Ceres and the fountain of grace."

"What desire you?"

"To be carried faster and farther than man can run or beast gallop."

The trampling sounds closed in. Shea smelled damp horse, and the next flash showed that the voices belonged to centaurs, led by one with a grizzled beard. He said: "Belphegor of the mountains, we know you by all names, but who is this? Is it our mission to carry him as well?"

"Aye."

"Is he an initiate in the mysteries of wood, wold and fountain?"

"Nay, not that I wot on. But that am I, and he a friend in need."

"Whee-he-he-he! We are forbid by an oath more dreadful than death to take none but those who have reached the degree of the three great mysteries."

"Hey!" shouted Shea. Another flash had shown him the three Paladins, leading their mounts more accurately in his direction than one would have believed possible. "What's this? Those lugs'll be here in a couple of minutes."

"There be rituals and vows through which all must pass who seek to live by the forest ways, Sir Harold," said Belphegor. "A thing of many days."

"Okay, skip it. I'll shin up a tree and hide."

"Nay, not from Duke Astolph's magic. One blast of that great horn, and you'd come tumbling like a ripened nut. Will you stand, then? My bow is useless in this wet, but we have made compact, you and I, and will guard your bare side with my hunting knife."

"It won't work, kid," said Shea, "even though it is damn

white of you." The pursuers were a bare two hundred yards away. Astolph had the big sword out, and the lightning-flash was reflected from it. Then inspiration reached him. "Wait a minute, I used to be a boy scout, and I had to pass an examination and take vows for that. Would that get me by?"

"What says he?" asked the bearded centaur. "I know not the chapter, yet—" Shea snapped out a brief account of the organization and the merit badge he had won in woodcraft, looking over his shoulder. Two or three centaur heads came together, and the bearded one returned. "It is believed that we can lawfully take you, man, though this is the first we hear of such wonders, and your craft be that of the small things. Mount!"

Before he had finished the sentence, Belphegor had vaulted lightly onto his back. Shea scrambled somewhat less gracefully onto the back of the other centaur, finding it wet and slippery.

"Ayoi! Ready, brother?" asked Shea's mount, pawing with its front feet.

"Ready. Whee-hee-hee!"

"Whee-he-he-he!" The centaur began to bounce, and as Shea, unused to this kind of ride, wiggled on its back, turned around: "Put your arms around me and hold on," it said.

Shea nearly released his grip in surprise as the first long bound was taken and a shout came from behind. It was a female centaur.

He looked over his shoulder. The last flash showed the pursuing paladins before they were hidden among the trees. The hippogriff, its feathers bedraggled, looked more melancholy than ever, and its expression would remain with him all his days.

CHAPTER 10

THE CENTAURS HALTED UPON A SMOOTH knoll. Behind them rose the slopes of the western Pyrenees, and before them the country rolled and flattened away into the high plateau of Spain. The sun was just pinking the crests.

"Here we rest," said Belphegor's centaur. "We cannot take you further, for lo! the Amir's camp is in sight, and our forests lie behind."

Shea slid off—legs stiff, eyes red, behind feeling as though it had been paddled, and teeth as furry as chows. Belphegor came down lightly on the balls of her feet, increasing Shea's already vast admiration for his wife. They thanked the centaurs, who waved farewell and galloped off as though their all-night run had been merely a warm-up, sending their "Whee-he-he-he!" after the travellers.

Shea turned in the other direction and shaded his eyes. Through the early-morning haze he could just see a village with white walls and flat roofs three or four miles off. And away beyond it, a patch of little tan humps would be the tents of Agramant, Commander of the Faithful.

Shea gave Belphegor a long, searching look, noting how fresh she seemed after an all-night ride.

"Is the chivalry of your land to stare?" she asked coolly.

"Sorry. I was just wondering what made you sort of— hold up and change your mind about your name. Last night, when the centaurs asked you."

A tiny frown appeared between her brows. "In sooth, I know not. 'Twas as though a veil were drawn, and I swam between worlds with my tongue framing words spoken by another."

"I can clear that up so it won't happen again."

"Nay, no more of your spells, Sir Magician. I lay it upon you as a condition of this adventure we undertake, that you

89

attempt no enchantments on me for whatever purpose." She looked at him earnestly, but her regard faded into a small yawn.

"Oh—all right," said Shea ruefully. "Wouldn't take much of an enchantment to put you to sleep though, now would it?"

"Marry, that shaft is not far from the clout. Could I but find a grove!" She looked around. "But this country is bare as a priest's poll."

"Shucks, why don't you try sleeping in a bed again?"

"Again? I have never—"

Shea suppressed a grin. "Sure, sure, I know. But lots of people do without dying of it, you know, and it even gets to be fun after a while." He looked towards the village. "There ought to be an inn in that town, and we'll have to go there anyway if we're going to stand any chance of finding Roger."

Amiably doubtful, she fell in beside him as he led the way down the slope to where a track took them toward the village. The matter still hung in abeyance when they reached the place, which did have an inn. This was a small house that differed from the private dwellings only by having a dry bush affixed over the door.

Shea banged with the hilt of his sword. Above, the shutters of a window swung outward. A villainous-looking head peered out to look in astonishment at the unshaven man in Saracen costume and the red-golden-haired girl with a longbow. Presently the proprietor appeared at the door, scratching himself under a leather jerkin whose laces were not yet tied. The request for breakfast and lodging seemed to depress him.

"O lord of the age," he said, "know that neither in this village nor for miles around is there so much food as would satisfy a sparrow, save in the camp of the Amir Agramant, on whose sword be blessings."

"Heigh-ho," said Belphegor, "then sleep we supless and dine our souls on dreams." She yawned again.

The innkeeper looked more lugubrious. "On my head and eyes, Allah preserve me from your displeasure, lady; but there is lacking in my poor house a place where such a moon of delight as yourself may companion with her lord. For behold, I have neither secluded alcoves nor a bath for the performance of the Wuzu ablution."

The girl's foot began to tap dangerously. However, Shea averted the storm by saying: "Don't let it worry you. We really want to sleep; and besides we're Christians, so the bath doesn't matter."

The landlord looked at him with an expression of cunning. "O man, if ye indeed be Christians, then there is nothing for it but you must pay ten dirhams before entering, for such is the regulation of the prince of this place, who is none other than that light of Islam, the Lord Dardinell."

Shea hearing the girl catch her breath slightly, remembered that Dardinell was the name of the man who had brought the poetic Medoro to her attention. It also occurred to him that the innkeeper was probably lying, or cheating him, or both. To these peasant-village characters, a member of an out-group was fair game. . . . Shea, becoming annoyed, reached into the twist of the cloth belt where he had put the remainder of the coins Chalmers had given him. He pulled out a handful—a small handful.

"Listen, pickle-puss," he said menacingly, "I haven't got time to argue with you, and the lady is tired. You take these and give us a place to sleep, or you can take a piece of this." He indicated the sword.

"Hearing and obedience," mumbled the innkeeper, dropping back a couple of steps. "Enter, then, in the name of Allah the Omnipotent."

The entry was dark and somewhat smelly, with a set of stone steps going up to the right. The innkeeper clapped his hands twice. A door opened at the rear, and a very black Negro, so small as to be a dwarf, and naked to the waist, scuttled in. He grinned from ear to ear, and the speed with which he came suggested that he had overheard some of the conversation. The innkeeper did not seem to like his cheerfulness, for he fetched the dwarf a crack on the ear that sent him spinning against the wall, and said: "O miserable buffoon, cease from mockery! You shall conduct these guests to the upper room and provide them with coffee of the night, as is the custom, for they have been long abroad and desire to sleep the day."

The dwarf got up, rubbing ear and cheek with one hand, and wordlessly motioned Belphegor and Shea up the stairs. The room at the top ran the whole width of the inn. It held ten beds like very low couches, only a few inches off the floor and covered with thin and moth-eaten Oriental rugs.

Belphebe looked at them with distaste. "Sir Harold, I know not how men can bear such shabby habitation, when they may live among clean trees."

She began to pace the floor, looking out of one window after another.

"It could be better," Shea admitted. "But anyway, we won't get rained on. Come on, kid, try it for once."

He yawned. The dwarf came trotting upstairs with a brass tray holding two little cups from which floated the appetizing smell of coffee. He set it on one of the beds, then bowed low. More out of the habit of tipping than anything else, Shea fumbled one of the odd-shaped coins and held it out. The little black man half-reached toward it, looking at Shea's face as though he suspected him of playing a joke in questionable taste.

"Go on, take it," said Shea. "It's for you. Honest."

With a snatch it was in the dwarf's hands, and he rolled over and over, holding the precious thing before his eyes and gurgling with delight. Shea picked up the coffee and took a long pull, then almost gagged. It was so cloyingly sweet as to be almost syrup. He asked Belphegor: "Is all the coffee like that around here?"

" 'Tis coffee. What else would you have?" she said, sipping her own.

"Why, you know how I like . . ." He checked himself; no use starting the same old argument with a real amnesiac, and it would only antagonize her. He amended: "I'd have a lot else. Hey, George!"

The dwarf, having ceased his antics, came trotting over to duck his head three times. Shea asked: "Have you got any of this stuff without sugar in it?"

The servitor seemed to be overtaken by some inner ill, for he put both hands to his belly and rocked from side to side, pointed to the cups and put both hands beneath one ear, then closed his eyes; jumped up, ran to the window and went through the motion of leaping out, then pointed to Shea.

"What's the matter?" asked Shea. "Can't you say anything?"

For answer the little man only opened his mouth and pointed again. He had no tongue.

"That's too bad, George." Shea turned to the girl. "What's he trying to put over?"

She gave a tired little laugh. "Meseems he would convey

that this be a brew so potent another cup would make one leap from a height. Marry, the one will not affect me so." She set down her cup, raised a small hand over another yawn, picked out one of the less dirty beds, and stretched out on it.

"Me, either," said Shea. It was too much trouble to argue. He stretched out on another; it might be straw under the disintegrating rugs, but his weary muscles found it softer than down. "Sweet dreams, kid." At least the fact that there was a multitude of beds precluded any silly arguments about laying his sword down the middle, as in the medieval romances. Though if a man were too feeble to climb over. . . .

Just as he was whirling down into the pool of sleep it occurred to him that maybe the dwarf was trying to let them know that the coffee was doped, but he forgot before he could do anything about it. . . .

Somebody was shaking him, and the side of his face stung with the memory of a slap. That goddam innkeeper! "Lay off!" he growled, his head fuzzy, and wriggled from the grasp. Slap!

This was too much. Shea rolled to his feet and started to swing; or tried to, for his arms were instantly pinioned from behind. Clearing eyes showed that he was in the center of a circle of armed Saracens. In another and larger group, some of whom turned as he came erect, he caught the sheen of Belphegor's bright hair, now mussed. Two of them were holding her. One had a black eye; the other had lost his turban, and his face bore an interesting criss-cross pattern of scratches.

"O my lord," said the innkeeper's voice from well in the rear, "did I not warn you that these were indeed Franks, and violent?"

"Verily, you are a mountain of wisdom," said a commanding voice. "What shall be your reward for having at once provided a pearl beyond price for my couch and an arm of the best for my battle?"

"Lord, I ask no more than the sunlight of your favor, and the payment of my proper reckoning. This unlucky Frank keeps the gains he has doubtless made from the robbery of true believers in his belt."

The owner of the commanding voice turned: a tall man with an unpleasant, dish-shaped face. "Seek if this be so," he ordered one of the men holding Shea. The latter, seeing that it would do no good to struggle, refrained from doing so.

"Verily, Lord Dardinell," said the one who was robbing him, "he has fourteen dirhams and a half."

"Give them to the innkeeper," said Lord Dardinell, and, turning back to that worthy, added: "You shall surely wait upon me in my tent after the hour of the second prayer tomorrow, when I shall have made proof of this Frankish damsel. If she prove a filly, as you have declared, your reward shall be ten times this amount; but if not, then only the double."

"Hey!" shouted Shea. "You can't do that. She's my wife!"

One of Shea's holders hit him across the face as Dardinell, expression going glum, turned to the girl. "Is this indeed the truth?" he demanded.

Before she could answer, another voice, somewhat high-pitched, spoke up: "O Lord Dardinell, it cannot be. When lately we saw this damsel at Castle Carena, she was surely neither wife nor widow, but a free maid of the forest, the inspiration of poetry."

Dish-face ran a tongue around red lips. "There is but one resource," he said, "and that is to smite the head of this dog of a Frank from his body, so that if wived, the damsel shall be widowed."

"Yet it is written," said the other voice, which Shea noticed belonged to an olive-skinned young man with delicate features, "that one shall not deal unjustly even with unbelievers, lest it be held against you at the last day. It is also lawful that even if the damsel be widowed this very day, the three-day ceremony of purification is necessary before one shall go in unto her. Therefore I say, my lord, that we should hold them both in a secure place until a learned Kazi can find the line of truth among these thickets. Moreover, O Prince of warriors, was it not your own word but now that here was a good arm to the service of the Prophet, on whose name be peace? Yet of what avail the arm without a head to guide it?"

Lord Dardinell put a hand to his chin and bowed the spiked helmet surmounted by a crescent. "O Medoro," he said finally, with somewhat ill grace, "you argue more finely than a doctor of law, and in a manner to make one believe that your own eyes are set on the damsel. Yet I can find small flaw in your doctrine." Shea, who had been holding his breath, let it out in a long *whoosh,* and the other Saracens murmured approval.

Dardinell stepped over to Shea and felt his biceps. "How came you hither, Frank?" he asked.

Shea said: "I had a little run-in, you might say, with some of the Emperor's paladins." That ought to put him in the best light, and had the advantage of being true.

Dardinell nodded. "Are you a fighter of proved worth?"

"I've been in a few scraps. If you'd like a little demonstration, just turn me loose from this gent holding my right arm . . ."

"That will not be needed. Will you faithfully serve the Amir Agramant in this war?"

Why not? Shea felt he owed nothing to the Paladins, while consenting would at least keep him alive long enough to figure out something. "Okay. Bring on your dotted line. I mean, I'll swear to uphold your just and merciful Amir and all that, et cetera, so help me Allah."

Dardinell nodded again, but added severely: "It is not to be thought that even if the Kazi decides that your marriage to this damsel be lawful, you shall retain ownership in her, for it is my wish that you pronounce upon her the formula of divorcement. Yet if you bear yourself well, I will give you sixteen others from the spoils, with faces like full moons. How are you named?"

"Sir Harold Shea."

"Sir Harr al-Sheikh. Hear a wonder: he bears both Nazarene and Muslim titles! How became you a chieftain?"

"I inherited it," said Shea ambiguously. "You know, border family," he added, remembering the Carenas. He felt easier as the grip on his arms relaxed. No, he decided looking around, there was no chance of getting the jump on the situation and releasing Belphegor. Too many of these guys had sharp-looking scimitars in their hands.

Lord Dardinell appeared to have lost interest in him. "Let the maiden be bound, but lightly, with silken cloths," he ordered. "O Medoro, you shall take this new warrior into your troop and see him armed; and your courage shall be responsible for his."

As the girl was led past, she looked toward Medoro instead of him, and Shea's heart ached. At the street a number of horses were tied, one of which was held for him to mount. It was a damn shame that there was no chance of going back for one crack at that innkeeper, but that would have to wait until more important things were cleaned up.

Shea winced as he climbed into the saddles, for his crotch-muscles were as hard as cables after the long centaur-ride. But they soon loosened under the rugged massage of the high saddle, and Shea was able to go along with only nominal discomfort.

As the cavalcade set off through a hot sun that had already passed noon, it occurred to Shea that it would take something more than magic to make his wife try sleeping in a bed again after this.

CHAPTER 11

TENTS WERE PITCHED IN ALL DIRECTIONS with a maddening disregard of order. Over the whole brooded a smell suggesting that the sanitary arrangements were primitive. Muslims of every size and complexion wandered among the tents, though there was little about them to suggest that this was an army. In fact, it looked more like an imitation Oriental bazaar at a big fair. Little groups argued and haggled over bargains or just argued; men lay asleep, ignoring the flies that crawled over them; from somewhere came the banging that might mean a smith. As the cavalcade picked its way among the tents, the arguers stopped arguing and some of the sleepers sat up to watch.

They made audible and highly personal comments on Belphegor. Shea felt his own face burning and began to invent a long series of ingenious tortures for them. However, she held her head high, paying no attention as she was carried past sidesaddle on a led horse. She had not so much as spoken to Shea since their capture. He did not blame her, remembering how much his fault it had been for not being careful about that scoundrelly innkeeper and for failing to interpret the dwarf's warning aright. It was certainly a poor payoff for the way she had got him out of a jam to dump her into one like this. Still, the question was . . .

Medoro touched his arm: "We ride this way," and led off to the left, followed by three or four of the group. Presently they arrived before a large striped tent, before which stood a pole from which hung what looked like the tail of a horse. Medoro dismounted and flung open the flap. "Will you enter, O Harr?"

Inside it was at least cooler than on the road. Medoro motioned toward a pile of carpets near the cloth partition

97

that divided this outer room from another, and sat down cross-legged on another pile adjoining. As far as Shea, no expert on Oriental ruggery, could judge, they were very expensive specimens. The young man clapped his hands, and then said to the scraggly-bearded servitor who appeared from within: "Bring bread and salt. Also sherbets."

"To hear is to obey," said the man, and ducked out. Medoro stared moodily at the carpet in front of him for a minute, then said: "Will you have a barber? For I perceive that you follow the Frankish custom of shaving the face, even as I myself, and are long from the pleasure of this cleanliness."

"It might be a good idea," said Shea, feeling his rasp-like chin. "Say, tell me, what are they going to do with her?"

"It is written that the tree of friendship may grow only beside the fountain of security," said Medoro, and lapsed into silence again until the servitor returned, followed by two more. The first carried a ewer of water and an empty basin. As Medoro extended his hands over the latter, the servitor poured water on them and then produced a towel. Then he performed the same service for Shea, who was glad to get off a little of the grime.

The second man had a tray on which stood something that looked like a flannel waffle, with a little dish of salt. Medoro broke off a piece of the waffle, sprinkled a pinch of salt on it, and thrust it toward Shea's face. The latter reached for it, but Medoro skillfully avoided his fingers and poked the morsel closer. Shea inferred that he was supposed to open his mouth; when he did so Medoro popped the object in and waited expectantly. It tasted fierce. As something more seemed to be expected, Shea in his turn broke off a piece of the flannel waffle, salted it, and returned the favor. The servitor disappeared. Medoro picked up his bowl of sherbet and sighed heartily.

"In the name of Allah, the Almighty, the Gracious," he said, "we have partaken of bread and salt together and have no harm towards each other. I have written a poem on that theme; would it broaden your bosom to hear it?"

The poem was long and, as far as Shea was concerned, did not make much sense. Medoro accompanied himself on a goose-necked lute he picked up from behind the rugs, caterwauling his refrain in a series of minors. Shea sat, sipping his sherbet (which turned out to be merely fresh orange-juice) and waiting. In the midst of one of the refrains there came a squalling of many voices outside. Medoro flung down his lute, seized up one of the smaller rugs, and rushed outside for the afternoon prayer.

When he returned he flopped down on the rugs again. "O Harr, verily you sheikhs of the Franks know no more of the spirit of life in Allah, whose Prophet is the True and Indubitable, than a pig knows of the nuts whereon it feeds. Yet you shall now tell me nothing less than the truth: are you indeed an approved warrior?"

Shea thought that one over for a moment. "How the hell do I know?" he said finally. "I've done a little fighting when I had to, but I've never been in a regular formal battle, if that's what you mean."

"Aye. On bread and salt I cannot conceal it; I am myself as a stick in the sand. None dare love me but for my verses alone; yet I am of great family, and nothing less than the tradition of might will serve."

He picked up the lute again and struck a few melancholy chords. "May I be forgiven," he said languidly, "and let it not be borne overlong against me on the Day of Days. The Lord Dardinell said nothing less than that you were to be armed. Are you one of those Franks who will strike with the lance?" He brightened momentarily. "I have composed a poem on the subject of blood. Would your soul be soothed to hear it?"

"In a while, maybe," said Shea. "Don't you think we ought to get this arming business over with first, chum? Lord Dardinell will be coming around on a tour of inspection, and I don't think it would look good."

"Ah, Allah, deliver me from this life whose weight is irksome to me!" said Medoro, and without appearing to exert himself threw the lute across the tent, so that Shea heard it crack against some solid obstruction on the far side. Medoro, after a moment of silence, clapped his hands and ordered the thin-bearded servitor: "Summon my armorer."

The armorer was a squat, brawny man with black hair clipped close and black eyes. Shea judged he might be a Basque like Echegaray, but he spoke in the manner of the Muslims: "Will the wonder of the centuries deign to stand? Ha, hum; I have a suit of mail that may fit the Light of the

East, but how will you be weaponed: A target, ha, hum. No doubt your magnificence will wish a scimitar also?"

"If you have a small straight sword with a point, it will do me swell," said Shea. Medoro appeared to have gone to sleep, with his mouth in a determined pout.

"O Sheikh Harr," said the armorer, "there may be such a weapon among the booty of Canfrano, but it is not to be hidden that these Frankish blades fail to hold the edge."

"Let's see one anyway. If it won't do, I'll take the longest and straightest scimitar you can find. With a point, too."

"May Allah strike me dead if you be not one of those who use the thrusting stroke! My father, who was smith before the Prince of Hind, has spoken of such in that land, but never have mine eyes been delighted by beholding such a one."

Medoro opened his eyes, clapped his hands, and told his valet: "Another lute, and tell the cook to set forth meats for the evening meal of my guest."

"Aren't you going to eat too?" asked Shea.

"My breast is straightened. I will dine on the food of thought." He took the new lute, struck it a couple of times, and gave vent to a long, howling note like that of a pin scratched across a window-pane.

The smith was still fussing and bowing. "It is revealed to me, O lord of the age," he said, "that there will be need for mail of unusual strength both on the shoulder and the upper arm—"

Medoro set down the lute. "Begone!" he shouted. "Master of noise, whose mother was mistress to a pig! Make your vile armor if you must, and send it here, but in silence."

As the smith scuttled out and the servitor began placing dishes before Shea, the young man relapsed into his playing and singing. It was not the ideal accompaniment to a meal. Shea managed as best he could the sticky mess before him without a fork; it was heavily spiced, but he was too ravenous to let that bother him. Coffee was brought, of the same appalling sweetness as that at the inn. Medoro laid aside his music to accept a cup. As he lifted it delicately to his lips, Shea said:

"What's eating you so, anyway? You act as though you'd lost your last friend."

"Nay," said Medoro, "I have found one, but—" he put down the cup, picked up the lute again, and sang:

"Ah, bittered is the heart
Which with all love must part;
The sun declines, and as it sinks
The tears from out my eyeballs start."

Although Shea was not overwhelmed by the pathos of
the poetry, Medoro laid down the lute and began to sob.

"Pull yourself together, pal," said Shea. "Is it about our
friend Belphebe—Belphegor, I mean?"

" 'Tis true. Spake you sooth when you said she was your
wife? Or was that a ruse to balk my lord Dardinell?"

"Well," said Shea, "that's a long and complicated story . . ."

"Nay, fear not to open your soul to your comrade of
bread and salt. True friendship is above the base weakness of
jealousy, as says the philosopher Iflatun."

Shea calculated his reply with the care of a sharp-
shooter. "I've known the girl for some time. But as for the
rest of it, her status now is exactly what it was when you
met her at Castle Carena. Doesn't that make you feel better?"
When Medoro only sighed gustily, Shea added: "I should
think we could hire a lawyer or something—"

"Verily, Sheikh Harr," interrupted Medoro, "your understanding is darkened. Know that the Kazi will surely decide
that it is lawful for the Lord Dardinell to go in unto the
damsel; for if you pronounce not the formula of divorce, he
will cause her to do so himself. Ah, what have I done that
a mere woman should bring this sorrow upon me? It was
clear that with hair of gold-red she would be of ill-omen.
Woe's me! I have but delayed the inevitable hour for the
three days of purification."

Shea said: "Anyway, I can tell you that anybody who
tried to make proof of our girl-friend without her consent
has got his work cut out for him."

But Medoro's tears were flowing again. Shea sat back,
thinking furiously. This twerp was about as much use as a
third leg, though Shea tried to be fair, balancing his natural
jealousy of Medoro's libido towards Belphegor against the
fact that the youth had, in a manner of speaking, saved
Shea's life at the inn. However, Medoro knew the rules, and
there was one resource which he had not yet exploited: his
own knowledge of magic.

"Where have they got her?" he asked.

"Nowhere but in the harem-tent of Lord Dardinell."

Said Shea: "Do you know whether Roger—you know, the one from Carena—has joined the army?"

The Saracen's woebegone expression changed to one of fine contempt. "It has reached me that the misbegotten son of a whore is indeed among us."

"You don't like him, then?"

"By Allah, if a cup of water would save him from Hell, I would give him fire to drink. At Castle Carena but lately, when I was reciting my stanzas in lament of Farragus, which is the best and longest poem I have composed, he snatched the lute from my hands."

For the first time Shea felt a certain sympathy with Atlantès' bull-like nephew. However, he said: "Okay, then, I need Roger in my business. Specifically, I want to kidnap him and get him back to Carena. You help me do it, and I think I can show you how to get Belphegor out of hock."

The handsome face distorted into lines of fear. "O Harr, Roger is so potent that no ten could stand against him. In Allah alone is protection, but we two would be to him as mice before an eagle."

"Take it or leave it," said Shea coolly. What he really wanted was to get Belphegor out of there and never mind the small change, but the chances of restoring his wife's Belphebe memory were not too good unless he could get her to Chalmers, with the latter's superior knowledge both of psychiatry and of magic. If Medoro just wouldn't play, however, he could back down at the last moment.

Someone howled at the door of the tent. The servant scampered through, and returned presently with a package that proved to contain the arms. Shea examined them while Medoro remained sunk in gloomy thought. The sword, while still a curved saber with most of the weight toward the point, was straighter than most, and the smith had ground a fine needle-point to it. There was also a spiked steel cap with a little skirt of chainmail to protect the neck, a dagger, a small round shield of brass hammered thin, and a mail shirt.

Shea laid them down and turned to Medoro. "Well?"

The young Saracen looked at him craftily. "O Lord Harr, how lies it in your power to perform things for which half this army were not enough?"

"You just leave that to me." Shea grinned. "I'll give you a hint, though; I know something about magic."

Medoro touched both sets of finger-tips to his temples,

and said: "There is no God but God, and it is written that none shall die before the appointed hour. Speak, and I will obey as though I were your Mameluke."

"Will Roger come here if you ask for him?"

"Nay, he would rather whip my slave from his door."

"Then we'll have to go to him. Do you know where he hangs out?"

"It is even so."

"Okay. But we won't do it just yet. I'm merely laying out the program. How much authority do you have around here?"

"O Sheikh, under Lord Dardinell I am captain of four-score men."

Shea thought it would go hard with a Saracen army if it had to rely on captains like this languishing lady-killer to lead it, but just now he was too busy to pursue that question. "Can you bring them here, three or four at a time?"

"Hearing and obedience," said Medoro, who salaamed and began to get up.

Shea, who did not altogether like the scared look that persisted in Medoro's eyes, said: "Hold it; let's have just one to start with. We can try out the magic on him to make sure it works."

Medoro re-seated himself and clapped his hands. "Bid Tarico al-Marlik enter and stay not, on the value of his head," he told the servant. Picking up the lute, he began to strum chords, the jewels in his bracelets flashing in the light of the Greek lamp that had been brought in with dinner.

"Lend me one of those bracelets, will you? asked Shea. When the guardsman came in, Shea had Medoro order him to sit down and relax, then placed the lamp before the soldier. As the young Saracen continued to pick the lute, Shea dangled the bracelet before the soldier's eyes, twirling it this way and that, meanwhile repeating in a low voice as much as he could remember of the sleeping-spell Astolph had used on him.

Either as magic or as hypnotism the method was a little unorthodox; it seemed to work nevertheless. The man's eyes went blank, and he would have tumbled over if he had not been leaning against the wall of the tent.

Presently Shea said: "Can you hear me?"

"Aye."

"You will obey my commands."

"As the commands of a father."

"The Amir wants to surprise the camp. Discipline needs tightening up. Do you understand?"

"It is as my lord says."

"As soon as the evening prayer is over, you will draw your sword and run through the camp, cutting tent-ropes."

"To hear is to obey."

"You will cut all the tent-ropes you can, no matter what anyone says to you."

"To hear is to obey," repeated the soldier.

"You will forget all about this order till the time for action comes."

"To hear is to obey."

"And you will forget who gave you this order."

"To hear is to obey."

"Wake up!"

The man blinked and came out of it, wiggling as though his foot had gone to sleep. As he stood up, Shea asked: "What were your orders?"

"To watch well the door of Lord Dardinell's tent tonight. But as my head lives, Lord Medoro has given me none others."

"He forgot. You were to send in four more men. Isn't that right, Medoro?"

"It is as has been spoken," said Medoro languidly.

The man shifted his feet. "There was—"

"Nothing else," said Shea firmly. He looked at Medoro, who laid down his lute and stared back.

"Verily, Sheikh Harr," said the latter, "this is as though the prophets were again on earth. Will he assuredly cut the tent-ropes as you commanded?"

"If he doesn't, I'll put a spell on him to make him eat his own head," said Shea, who had decided that he could count on all the coöperation the twerp was capable of giving. "Listen, when those others come in, keep it up with that Oriental swing, will you? I think it has something to do with putting them under."

CHAPTER 12

WHEN THE LAST OF THE FOURSCORE GUARDS had been given his orders, Shea felt tired. Medoro, placing a delicately-formed hand over his mouth, said: "Surely we have now done so much that the darkness of Eblis must fall on the camp, and we can easily seize the damsel and make off with her. I am wearied, though somewhat comforted by the excellence of your plan. Let us sleep and await the deliverance of Allah."

"Nothing doing," said Shea. "In my country we have a proverb about Allah's helping those who help themselves, and there's one thing we've got to help ourselves to right now. That's Roger. Remember, you promised." He stood up, put on the steel cap, buckled on the sword and stuck the sheath of the dagger through the sword-belt. The mail-shirt, he decided, would have to stay behind, since for the kind of work he envisaged it was important to keep down weight. Medoro sulkily imitated him.

Outside the shadows were already stretching across the valley below the slope that held the encampment. Although Shea did not know when the hour of evening prayer was, he guessed it would be soon. That meant they must hurry if they wanted to catch Roger as part of the combined operation. Once the bruiser got loose with an uproar going on there would be no finding him.

But Medoro only sauntered along, possessed of a perfect demon of slowness. Every now and then he stopped to give or acknowledge a greeting, and those to whom he spoke seemed all to want to start an interminable discussion of nothing.

Shea thought these must be the most garrulous people on earth. "Listen," he said finally, "if you don't come along, I'll put a spell on you that will make you challenge Roger to a duel."

Shea had heard of people's teeth's chattering, but this was the first time he had actually heard it. Medoro mended his pace.

Roger, it appeared, lived in a tent of Spartan simplicity as to outline, but as big as Medoro's. Two fierce-looking bearded men were pacing back and forth in front of it with naked scimitars.

"We want to see Roger of Carena," said Shea to the nearest. The other paused and joined his companion, who was examining the callers.

The first guard said: "There are many tents in the camp. Let the lords seek another, since all are friends under Allah." He held his sword about waist-high, just in case.

Shea glanced over his shoulder to see the sun sinking fast. "But we've got to see him before the evening prayer," he insisted, shaking off the fingers Medoro was plucking at his sleeve with. "He's a friend of ours. We knew him in Carena."

"O Lord, the Prince Roger's withers will be wrung. Yet it is written that it is better that one man should have an unhappiness, which endures only the appointed hour of God, than that two should lose their lives. Learn that if Lord Roger should be roused before the hour of evening prayer, we two should lose nothing less than our heads, for so he has sworn it by the hair of his beard."

"He hasn't got one," said Shea. Medoro, however, plucked insistently and whispered: "Now there is not help for it but we must leave this project for the other, since we are evidently not to be admitted by these two good men. Would you try steel against them and so provoke the shame of Islam?"

"No, but there's something else I'd try," said Shea, whipping round on his heel. Medoro followed him dubiously until they reached the side of the tent next door. With his dagger Shea cut eight long slivers of wood from one of the tent-pegs. Two of these he stuck under the brim of his helmet, so that they projected like horns, and two more he inserted under his upper lip, hanging down like tusks. Then he decorated Medoro's wondering face likewise with the remaining four.

That ought to do for what Doc Chalmers called the "somatic" part of the spell. As for the verbal part, how could he do better than Shakespeare, slightly modified for the occasion? Shea turned round and round on his heel, moving his hands in Chalmers' passes and chanting in a low voice:

"Black spirits and white, red spirits and gray,
Mingle, mingle, mingle, you that mingle may;
Fair is foul and foul is fair;
Change, O change the form we bear!"

"Okay," he said to Medoro; "come along."

They swung round the corner of the tent. The guard who had been talking to them was just facing their way. He took one look at them, gasped: "The Jann!", dropped his sword, and ran for his life. The other guard looked also, turned a curious mottled color, screamed: "The Jann!" Falling on the ground he tried to bury his face in the grass.

Shea lifted the flap and led the way boldly in. There was no light in the outer compartment, and it was already dim with exterior twilight, but there was no mistaking the mountain of flesh piled among the rugs. Shea started toward it, but in the darkness tripped over some small object. He pitched forward and, unable to stop himself, struck the mass of Roger in the midriff in the position of a man kneading a vast vat of dough.

Roger awoke at once, rolling to his feet with incredible speed. "La-Allah-il'-Allah!" he cried, snatching a huge scimitar from the wall of the tent. "Ha, Jann! I have not fought Jann!" The sword curved back for a blow as Medoro cowered away.

"Wait!" yelled Shea.

The scimitar checked. "Hold it a minute, will you?" said Shea. "We're really friends. I'll show you." He stepped over to Medoro, pronouncing the counter-spell and pulling at the chin-length tusks into which the slivers beneath Medoro's lips had turned.

Nothing happened. The tusks did not give. Between them Medoro still wore his foolish, frightened grin, and above, a pair of bull-like horns continued to project from neat holes in the young man's helmet.

Shea repeated the counter-spell again, louder, feeling of his own face and head, and discovering that he was likewise festooned with horns and tusks. Again, however, nothing happened.

Far away somewhere a voice rose in a banshee howl.

That would be an imam whose alarm-clock, or whatever he used for the purpose, was a little fast, calling the faithful to prayer. The others would soon follow.

Shea faced Roger and said: "Listen, let's talk this over. We're Jann, all right, sent here by the big boss to fight with the best mortal fighter in the world. But we have some pretty terrible powers, you know, and we want to arrange things so you don't have to put on a scrap at odds of more than two to one."

It sounded phony as hell in Shea's own ears, but Roger let the scimitar droop and grinned beefily. "By Allah the Omnipotent! The hour of good fortune has come upon me. Surely there would be no greater pleasure than to be with two of the Jann in battle bound."

Roger flung himself among the rugs, half-turning his back toward Shea, who motioned frantically to Medoro to sit beside the colossus. Shea hoped Medoro would keep doing what he did best, namely talking. The twerp was probably too scared to do anything else, for he flopped beside Roger, saying: "Among our people we have a poem of the combats of the Jann. Would your lordship care to hear it? If you have a lute—"

"O Jinn, I would hear it not much more than a poem about dogs pissing in the street. Learn that at Castle Carena I acquired the taste for the despisal of poetry, since the worst of all poets came among us to visit: Medoro by name."

Shea caught the glance of appeal and indignation which Medoro flashed over his shoulder through his jinn makeup, but continued to stroll about the tent, out of the conversation. A large dagger with an ornate gold-hilted handle hung on the wall; he hefted it by the scabbarded blade and looked at the back of Roger's head.

"Know, O Lord Roger," said the poet rapidly, "that by poetry and song alone is the world advanced. For it is the rule of the Prophet, on whose name be blessings . . ."

A steel spike stuck up through the center of Roger's turban, meaning that he had on some kind of helmet beneath the cloth. If Shea hit him while he wore that, the dagger-hilt would merely go bong, and Roger would turn and grapple.

Medoro was talking a perfect flood of words that made little sense.

Shea reached down, gripped the spike firmly, and switched

it forward, tumbling helmet and turban both over the big man's face.

"Ho!" cried Roger's muffled voice as he reached upward.

Thump! The dagger-hilt hit his shaven poll in the medular region. Shea was left with the helmet-and-turban combination in his left hand as the ox rolled over and down. From outside came the united squalling of the call to prayer.

A thread of spittle ran down Medoro's chin beside the left tusk, and his hands fluttered wildly. "There—there is no gug-grace or goodness but in Allah," he babbled. "What thought is now to be taken for preservation?"

"Suppose you just leave that to me while you get busy and find some extra turbans. I haven't steered you wrong yet, have I?"

Medoro, familiar with camp life, quickly found the turbans in the inner compartment, and they tied Roger firmly, winding him round and round with them and knotting them until he looked like a coocoon. He seemed to be breathing all right; Shea hoped his skull were not fractured. Time was getting shorter and shorter, with the show outside about to begin.

Medoro said: "O Lord Harr, surely we shall never be able to move him hence, and what of the fearsome appearance you have put upon us?"

"Shut up," said Shea. "I'm thinking."

"If we had but the magic carpet of Baghdad—"

Shea snapped his fingers. "Right on the button! I knew I'd forgotten something. Here, find stuff that'll make a small fire with a lot of smoke. Is there a feather anywhere around here? Don't argue with me, damn it. This is important if you want to see Belphegor again."

When Medoro returned from the inner compartment of the tent with a few twigs and the aigrette of an ornamental turban, he found Shea already busily at work. The journeyman magician had caught a couple of the big blue flies that buzzed about in vast numbers, and looped a silken thread from Roger's wrappings about them, attaching one end of it to the fringe of Roger's main carpet. The flies tried to take off as he released them.

"Put those twigs in a little pile here and light them," Shea directed, rolling back the carpet to leave a bare space on the ground.

While Medoro made the light with flint and steel and a

tinder-box, Shea pulled the aigrette apart and began weaving it into the carpet, knotting it into the fringe. Outside something seemed to be going on. As the flame caught, shouts and the sound of running became audible.

The twigs, aromatics, filled the tent with a pungent smoke as Shea recited the spell he had been composing:

"Be light—*cough!*—carpet, as the leaves you bear;
Be light as the clouds that fly with thee.
Soar through the skies and let us now but share
The impulse of the strength. Let us be free
From—*cough! cough! cough!* If even
The Roc and all the Jann could fly like we
Then were they—*cough!* right aërial indeed.
To you the spirits of the sky are given
That they may help us in our sorest need.
Cough-cough-cough!"

The smoke died. The carpet was beginning to wiggle, parts of it rising from the ground and settling down again with a slight *whump*, while the tumult outside increased. The Jinn that was Medoro rubbed smarting eyes.

"O Sheikh Harr," he said, "this is not the worst of poetry, though it must be admitted that you failed to accompany it with the lute. Moreover there was a foot missing from the fifth line, and the end is somewhat weak."

"Never mind the higher criticism, but help me get this elephant onto the carpet, will you?" said Shea.

They rolled Roger over and wrapped him in one of the sitting carpets before depositing him on the—Shea hoped—flying one. His eyes had come open and regarded them balefully. Where the gag allowed, the muscles of his face moved in something like prayer.

Shea flung back the tent door and looked out. There was certainly something happening in the gathering dusk; people running in all directions with manifold shoutings. As Shea watched, a big square tent with a pennon on top, farther along the hillside, corkscrewed down into collapse.

"Sit down and hold on," Shea told Medoro. He himself climbed on the carpet, which seemed to be showing signs of restlessness even under Roger's weight. Reaching to his full height, Shea swung his sword at the roof, which split to show an indigo sky from which one solemn star winked back at him. He squatted and declaimed:

> "By warp and by woof,
> High over the roof—"

Chop! went a sword into one of the tent-ropes outside. Chop! went another. "Stand, in the name of Allah!" shouted a voice. Shea finished:

> "Fly swiftly and surely
> To serve our behoof!"

The tent collapsed, and the carpet swooshed up and out through the gap, its fringes flapping.

CHAPTER 13

A BAREHEADED MAN AND ONE OF SHEA'S rope-cutters were arguing so violently that neither noticed the carpet as it soared over their heads. Agramant's camp was in pandemonium beneath; everywhere tents were wobbling and collapsing. Some were as large as circus-tents, and great was the fall thereof. Lumpy objects moved under the enshrouding canvas, and here and there men fought. Out on one of the spurs of the hillside a tent had gone down into a fire which blazed brightly in the gathering gloom, while people ran around it, trying to beat out the flames or douse them with futile small buckets of water.

The carpet heaved and bucked, swirling this way and that. A little experiment showed Shea that he could direct its movements by pulling left, right, up, or down at the fringe of its leading edge. However, further experiment added the information that it was so very sensitive on the controls that he must be careful lest he throw them into a loop. Roger almost rolled off as the vehicle took a vicious downcurve. Medoro, though he had not eaten, seemed to be having trouble keeping whatever was in his stomach.

"Where is it?" shouted Shea.

Medoro pointed to one of the largest tents of all, well up on the slope, with a swarm of pennons floating from its multiple peaks. Dardinell's pavilion. Shea jerked at the fringe, and the carpet did a sweeping bank towards it.

The pavilion was a young city in itself. Besides the main tent, a score of lesser, outlying structures were connected to it by canopies. Among them the powerful figure of Dardinell himself could be seen among a group of officers on horseback who were trying to bring order into those on foot.

"Where's the harem?" demanded Shea. Medoro put one hand to his tusks to hold back a gulp, and with the other pointed toward an elongated tent that sprang from one side of the main structure.

As the carpet swooped, the sound of Shea's voice brought a face in their direction. There was a yell, the whole group flowered with faces, and a flung javelin went past. Before more could follow they were over the tangle of lordly tents and out of range. They sailed in toward the roof of the harem tent. As they did so, Shea, controlling the carpet with his left hand and some difficulty, whipped out his sword and made a twenty-foot gash in the fabric.

He then took the carpet around in a curve and back to the hole he had made. "Duck!" he said to Medoro. Aiming carefully, he drove for the hole, which had been widened by the tension of the ropes. One of Shea's horns caught the edge for a moment, then ripped through. They were inside.

They were in a room full of women, so little below that Shea could have joined hands with them by leaning over the edge. The women, however, did not seem in a mood to join hands; instead, they ran in all directions, screaming: "The Jann! The Jann!" Shea encouraged them by leaning over and gibbering a little.

The carpet moved smoothly to the nearest partitions and then stopped, its leading edge curling where it met the cloth, and its side edges flapping like some lowly marine organism. Shea reached out and slit the camel's hair across. The next room was a kitchen, empty save for the furniture of the trade. The next compartment held nothing but a pair of eunuchs throwing dice. These screamed in high voices, and one of them tried to crawl away under the outer edge of the tent, as Shea slit his way through the next wall.

"Damn maze," said Shea. The outer tumult of the camp had been dampened to a whisper by the many thicknesses of cloth. Two more partitions, both yielding empty rooms, and the coolth of the evening was once more on their faces. Shea could see a couple of soldiers afoot and a horseman running past, silhouetted against a fire further down the hill. He hastily manoeuvered the carpet around another curve and cut his way into the wall of the tent again. It was only the kitchen once more, and the whole structure of the tent seemed to be growing ricketty from the repeated slashings.

Nevertheless Shea warped his craft up to the kitchen's one unslit wall. A gash—and they had found their goal.

The room Lord Dardinell used for his more personal

pleasures was full of precious things. Over against the wall, under a hanging out of which eddied a slow smoke of incense, priceless cushions had been piled on priceless carpets to make one of the most elaborate beds Shea had ever seen. In the midst of these cushions a bound figure writhed.

Shea tried to bring the carpet to a halt by pulling up on his leading edge, but that only took him to the ceiling; by pulling down, but that only brought him to the floor. He considered trying to snatch the girl on the way past as a broncho-buster picks a handkerchief from the ground, but rejected the idea as too risky. One hand would be needed for the carpet, and Medoro was no help at all.

He came around the room in another curve and recited:

> "By warp and by woof,
> In the midst of the roof,
> To save the fair lady
> Stand still and aloof."

The carpet halted. It was a long way to the ground, and this would be no time to sprain an ankle. However, Shea, swung over the side, let himself down to his full length by gripping the yielding fringe, and dropped. He landed in the midst of the cushions on all fours, and got to his knees.

The figure on the bed rolled over and glared at him with furious eyes from under a disordered mop of graying hair, grunting through its gag.

"Eeek!" shrieked Medoro from above. "'Tis the Amir himself! We are surely at the last hour. There is no God but God."

And in fact it was indeed the Amir Agramant, Commander of the Faithful, Protector of the Poor, just and merciful Lord of Hispania, trussed, bound, and gagged with his own turban.

"By the mass! More magic!" said Belphegor's voice. Shea turned and saw her poised to spring at him, dagger in hand.

"Stop!" he said. "I'm Harold. Don't you know me?"

"A hornèd demon the lord of Shea? Nay but—and yet the voice—"

"Come on, you know me. This is just a gag; a magical gag. The other spook, up there on the rug, is your boyfriend Medoro. Now do you get it? We're here to save you."

"Nay, 'tis assuredly some trick. Come not nigh, or man or monster, your weasand will be slit."

"Medoro," called Shea. "She won't believe we're us. Make a poem for her, will you, chum?"

To judge by Medoro's expression, his muse was not in the best of fettle, but he valiantly cleared his throat and began in a whining voice:

> "We are not lost to prudence, but indeed
> Stand here bewildered. What shall be our rede?
> Since none will aid us from this tent to flee,
> By spells of great Lord Harr must we be free;
> But ah! my heart is lost and passion-spent;
> To none but Allah can we trust in need."

"Nay, I begin to trow," said Belphegor, her mouth losing its hard line. "This is Medoro's veritable voice which comes from the shaping. But what is now your counsel friends?"

"We're going out of here on that flying carpet, the way we came in," said Shea.

The girl stood on tiptoe and reached. "But how to attain it?"

"More turbans needed," said Shea, practically. "Where would they be?"

Belphegor leaped across the tent. "This chest—" and flung it open. Sure enough, it was filled with fine silk turban-cloths, neatly folded. He linked three of them together with solid square-knots and tossed one end up to Medoro, who caught it on the second try, and braced himself while Belphegor swarmed up it, light as a squirrel. Then Shea took a firm grip on the lowest knot and began to climb, but he had barely cleared the ground when the turban-rope went slack and he came down on his behind, the rope on his head.

"Hey!" cried Shea, stepping on the Amir and he stumbled to his feet. He saw Medoro, his jinn-eyes shifting as he crouched at the edge of the carpet and muttered. The edge of the carpet fluttered and it shifted position a little.

Shea would have said something else and more vigorous, but before he could get the words out, Belphegor leaned over the edge, with: "Throw up your end!" She caught it neatly, took a turn round her waist and called: "Mount, Sir Harold!"

Shea hesitated, afraid of pulling the girl off, for though

he did not doubt her strength, he weighed a hundred and sixty. But just at this moment a troop of eunuchs flung aside the curtain and came waddling into the room, pointing, yelling and waving scimetars at least a foot wide. He swarmed up the turban-rope clumsily but effectively as a thrown dagger tumbled past him.

"Get over and let a man run this thing!" he said to Medoro. He spoke to the carpet and they slid through the gap in the tent-wall, out into the rapidly descending twilight. The fire at one side of the camp was still burning; figures appeared to be dancing before it.

Shea jockeyed the carpet up to what he judged was an altitude safe from arrow-shot and turned to Medoro. "Well, what's the alibi? You better make it damn good."

"I—I—but friend Harr, let the shield of our bread and salt turn aside the sword of your anger. Truly is it said by Al Q'asun that he who sees into the hearts of many can seldom see into his own. Ah, most miserable of men!" He bent his head and the jewelled bracelets flashed as he beat his breast. "Your servant had no other thought but that when the end of the bond was lost, so much was lost that I should regret it to the end of days. But there is no might save in Allah, who has preserved you to be the delight of our eyes."

"You damn twerp," said Shea, through his teeth. "So you thought you'd sneak off and leave me and then make a poem about it. That's the idea, isn't it?"

"Nay, I am but a reed in the wind of your displeasure, and my breast is straitened, my brother," said Medoro, and reaching to the hem of his robe at the chest, gave it a little rip. (Shea noticed that it appeared to have been re-sewn several times; it was evidently a habit with the young man.) "Now there is no help for it but I must die." Two big tears rolled down his cheeks and stood gleaming on the tusks.

Belphegor put her arm around his shoulders. "Ah, unhappy wight, grieve not! Sir Harold, I charge you straitly that you shall not overbear him, for he is a troubadour, and I hold it somewhat less than knightly to treat him as less than one who has sustained you throughout this deed."

"Okay, okay," said Shea. "He's a hero and a pet. I just don't know why we bothered rescuing you at all. You were doing all right when we came in."

It was Belphegor's turn to be hurt, as Shea observed with a touch of vindictive relish. "Fie, for shame!" she said.

"If you'll magic me with your enchantments into the most ungrateful of wenches, I'll have my favor back."

Her nostrils moved and Shea, feeling suddenly wretched, turned to the business of navigation. It had been a splendid exploit, and they should all have been elated. Instead of which . . .

After a moment he got a grip on himself, realizing that he was being pretty immature in getting sore at Medoro, who was merely one of those schizoid types who can no more help disintegrating under stress than he, Shea, could help pulling himself together under similar circumstances. Aloud he said: "All right folks, I think we've done enough quarrelling for one night." (He realized that he had done most of the quarrelling, but he was also captain, and an apologetic attitude would undermine the position.) "Are we for Castle Carena?"

"My bow," said Belphegor. "I am undone without it. Perchance 'twill be at the inn where we were taken. Will you do me the grace to see, Sir Harold?" The voice was still chilly.

"Good idea," said Shea, trimming the carpet a trifle in the direction of the town. "I'd like to take a poke at that inn-keeper myself, and now I have the equipment." He stroked his tusks appreciatively.

Behind him he felt the girl shift herself gingerly on the yielding surface to a sitting position on the rolled-up rug that was Roger. A sound somewhere between a groan and a growl emerged; Belphegor leaped to her feet, making the carpet tip perilously. "What's here! Do carpets speak as well as move in your enchantments?"

Shea grinned over his shoulder. "That's your old boy-friend, Roger of Carena. We're taking him back to uncle."

"Verily?" She pulled back an edge of the rug and stared in the fading light, then gave a peal of silvery laughter. "Nay, this joys me much, and for this joy you are restored to favor as my true knight, Sir Harold. But I'd have one of the great bear's ears as a trophy." She whipped out her small hunting knife and the carpet heaved as Roger strove to wriggle in his bonds. Medoro's jinn-face took on a greenish cast. Shea said: "Cut it out, will you, girl friend? We're getting there."

The town was below them, lemon-colored gleams picking out the windows of the inn. Shea circled the carpet round the structure and carefully manoeuvred it up to one of the windows that lighted the upstairs dormitory, peering in. There seemed to be no sleepers, only a feeble oil-lamp on a low table.

"I don't see it," he said. "Where did you leave it?"

"I deemed I had laid it upon the bed next to my own, with my quiver," she said.

"Not there now. Medoro, you and I will have to do a little searching. Beautiful, you stay here and see that the carpet doesn't drift away from the window, because we may come back running and dive through. You can move it by pulling gently on the fringe here, but don't do it if you don't have to. If Roger makes a fuss you can have *both* his ears."

Medoro said: "Oh, my lord and brother, is it not more meet that I should wait, both as one who can defend this carpet from attack, and because I know not one bow from another?"

"No!" said Shea. "Come along."

He let himself carefully through the window, reaching up a hand to help Medoro. They scoured the dormitory from end to end, peering under carpets and in corners, but not a trace of archery-tackle.

"Inshallah!" said Medoro. "It was ordained from the beginning of the world that we should not . . ."

He broke off at the sound of approaching horses, and then of voices downstairs. Shea tiptoed to the head of the stairs. A voice was just saying: "Uncle, are there within your caravanserai certain fugitives from the justice of the Commander of the Faithful?"

"My head be your sacrifice!" came the voice of the innkeeper. "Were there such, I had long since delivered them to the servants of the Prince, straitly bound. But are there not other inns than mine?"

The owner of the other voice replied: "By Allah, our breasts are narrowed, and an enchantment lies upon this expedition for the abatement of the Nazarenes! For behold, Lord Dardinell must bring home to the camp a damsel with hair of ill-omen, a very Frank, who indeed aroused the jealousy of the sons of Satan the stoned. For with the setting of the sun what should befall but there came unto the camp an army of furious Jann, each taller than a tree and pinioned with four wings of brass, who spurned over our tents as though they had been toys. By the grace of Allah, few were slain, though many ran in panic, and we have come to recall those who fled, lest they be taken later and fire be applied to their feet so they may flee no more."

The innkeeper apparently turned around to show them into the lower rooms, for his voice became inaudible and there was a sound of feet. But a moment later he picked up again ". . . the apartments for sleeping, which be untenanted."

Medoro jerked at Shea's arm and cast an imploring glance toward the window. Shea got out his sword and putting his lips close to his fellow-jinn's ear, murmured: "Draw, and we'll scare the living bejesus out of them after that story he told. When I jump and yell, you do the same." He waved the weapon; Medoro produced and waved his own, though with somewhat uncertain gestures. The footsteps started up the stair; Shea leaped with a whoop, in time to see three soldiers, with the innkeeper behind them.

He must have looked a hundred feet tall, coming down from above, and behind him Medoro emitted a shrill yell that was even more blood-curdling than his own. An answering scream came from the men below, mingled with a clatter of dropped weapons and the sound of heavy bodies hurling themselves any old way toward escape. For a few seconds the bottom of the stair was a confused mass of trunks and limbs; then the soldiers fought their way loose and raced out the door.

The last one to get to his feet was the innkeeper, who as low man had been trampled by all three others. He was a little too slow on the getaway as hoofbeats diminished into the distance. Shea noted that he had both hands up for the formal tearing of his garments and his mouth open for a scream, but that both his motor nerves and his vocal seemed paralyzed.

He was not quite up to cutting the fellow down in cold blood, so he gave him a stiff left to the nose. The innkeeper dropped like an English heavyweight and rolled over, burying his face in his arms and awaiting the end.

"Look for that bow while I play footsie with this guy," said Shea, digging his toe into the innkeeper's ribs.

Medoro sidled past, his eyes rolling as though he expected Shea to begin carving steaks off the unfortunate man at any moment, but the latter contented himself with goosing the fellow tentatively with the point of the sword, until the young Saracen returned, waving the bow and saying: "By the omnipotence of Allah, it is indeed found!"

"Uncle, or whatever your name is," said Shea, "if you want to stay alive a little longer, lie where you are till you count slowly up to one hundred. Then you may get up and tell anybody you like about how the jann spared your life. Okay, Medoro."

As the carpet resumed its slightly undulating flight, Medoro inched forward and patted one of Shea's feet. "Know, O auspicious Lord Harr," he said, "that this is a deed worthy to be written in the most divine verse on tablets of silver with letters of gold. It is given to poets, in the name of the Prophet, on whose name be blessings, to know all that passes in the minds of men, and had I but a lute, I would compose verses—"

"Too bad you haven't got the lute," said Shea. "But right now I'm more interested in figuring out the shortest way to the Castle of Carena."

Belphegor pointed. "Sir Harold, it lies almost under the star of the Lion, thitherward. Behold that triad of bright stars; the lowest lies under the pole. And for your help in aiding Medoro to find my weapon, much thanks. It was knightly done to accompany him."

Shea, looking down at the broken ground where the shadows were now deep, guessed that they were making twenty to thirty miles an hour. As the rolling highlands gave way to swollen, solid peaks of mountain, he had to put his vehicle into a climb to avoid the crests. All three began to shiver in their light clothes, and Medoro's teeth rattled. Shea envied Roger the rug.

That gave him an idea. They must be far enough from Agramant's camp so that over those stony mountains it would take days for the Amir's men to catch up. Why not rest comfortably through the remainder of the night? He put the carpet into a glide toward a low rounded peak and set it down, murmuring (under his breath so that Medoro would not hear) a spell to keep it there.

The Roger-rug grunted again as the rear end of the carpet touched a stone. It occurred to Shea that there was no particular reason why the big man should be comfortable while Belphebe-Belphegor was cold that night, so the prisoner was unrolled from his rug; and then it occurred to him that it would be interesting to hear what Roger had to say, so he removed the gag.

The perfect chevalier had plenty to say, beginning by calling them offspring of Marids and one-eyed sows, then running up and down the chain of their ancestry and remarking that his uncle would have them pickled in brass bottles under the seal of Solomon. With academic interest Shea noted that the invective had a certain weakness toward the end. The slow brain of the big lummox had evidently not quite been able to resolve the contradiction of jann who spoke with the voices of Shea and Medoro.

The poet plucked at Shea's sleeve. "O brother," he said, "shall we not rather release him for the night; for it is contrary to the law of the Prophet that a man shall not be allowed to take his relievements. As is said by Abu Nowas—"

"As is said by myself, nothing doing," replied Shea. "I don't want to sit up guarding this big lug all night, and if Bradamant gets hold of him, he'll forget all about the law of the Prophet, anyway."

He was astounded to hear the big lug groan, and see a glistening tear on his eyelids in the star-shine; and even more astounded when Roger shut up completely.

Belphegor and Medoro moved a little apart and sat on a rock, talking softly and looking at the bright, near stars. Shea saw his arm go round the girl's waist and guessed he didn't dare try anything at this stage, and under the circumstances, there didn't seem to be much point in building a campfire. He pulled a twig from the top of a scrubby bush and bit down on it, trying to pretend that it was a pipe and recalling the ad for some brand of tobacco—"A gentleman's solace."

Solace! That was what he needed. What was the use, anyway, of this running across a parade of universes not even real and having nothing to show for it? What he ought to do was go back to Garaden, finish getting his doctor's degree, become a big-shot psychiatrist, consulted by alcoholics and the affluent screwy, and make money. With money you could have everything—even affection. He recalled a statistic that Garaden had itself gathered, to the effect that something over sixty per cent of women could be happy and affectionate with any really good provider.

It wasn't really as simple as that, though. That red-haired spearshaft of a girl over there was his wife, none genuine without this signature, and just any girl who wanted a good provider wouldn't take her place. Anyway, he had a responsibility. He had married her and promised to keep her safe—particularly from such things as the Medoro menace. He had seen the thing so often in case-histories: women of her forceful type, thoroughly competent as long as sex was left out, falling for good-looking weaklings whom they felt the impulse to mother, and unhappy because of it. They usually ended up by despising the men in question.

Well, what? He couldn't very well murder Medoro, that was not in the limits of his own *ethos*, and it would probably have the contrary effect on the girl than the one he wanted. It would fix the love-image in her memory forever as something desirable and lost. Moreover, he had no desire to bump off Medoro. The guy was perfectly frank about his own weakness as a fighter or man of action of any kind, no sham about him. He was only mis-cast as a Saracen warrior, like one of the Marx brothers trying to play Hamlet. With the right kind of stage-manager . . .

The whole problem was one to pass on to Chalmers, that very well integrated personality, who didn't mind tearing other people's lives apart to mend the details of his own.

Meanwhile, it would be a good idea to get some sleep. Medoro was supposed to watch Roger during the early part of the night. He hoped the idiot would not do anything stupid, like turning the perfect cavalier loose, but consoled himself with the thought that if Medoro did that, Roger would probably fall on the poet first and make enough racket to wake the other two up.

A wolf howled in the distance. Everybody moved, rustlingly at the sound. Another howl answered it. The howlers set up a duet, the howls became shorter and closer together, then they ceased. About that time Medoro began to croon in a minor key, presumably a poem of his own.

Lucky stiff, thought Shea, meaning the wolf.

CHAPTER 14

"NOW WHERE THE HELL ARE WE?" DEMAND-
ed Harold Shea.

Below the edge of the carpet nothing was visible but
rocky peaks, pine-clad slopes and steep gorges, with now
and then a metallic flash of water in them. "We've been
flying for hours, and all we get is more of the same. I think
we ought to stop at a gas station and ask."

A little frown came between Belphegor-Belphebe's lined
brows. "As oft erst, Sir Harold, I wot not—right well—
what you would say."

"It's like this; we seem to be a long time getting nowhere, and I could do with something to eat."

She looked at him, then glanced quickly sidewise and
down. "I marvel that you are so eager to end this, our adventure; yet since you will have it so, there lies a road now
below us which, an I mistake not, will lead us to Carena."

"You have the damndest eyes, kid. Where?"

She pointed. It was a mountain track like two or three
they had glimpsed already, snaking down one side of a
gorge, across a stream by stepping-stones, and up the opposite slope.

Shea banked and spiralled down toward the track. Belphegor indicated four dots ahead on the road which, as they
approached, resolved into a man leading three laden asses.
Shea slid in toward him, and just above head level, called:
"Hi, there!"

The man looked up, his whole face seemed to dissolve,
he gave a squawk of terror and began to run, the asses
rocking behind him. The carpet zipped past a hairpin turn
and came round in a long curve as Shea brought it back,
crying to the girl: "You talk to him!"

"Nay, hold rather," she said. "He is so sore affrighted
with your grim aspect that an you clip him close, he'll but
leap a cliff and take the known death rather than the terror
unknown."

"Allah upon you if you do!" said Medoro. "This is most excellent sport to see a merchant so buffooned."

"No, she's right," said Shea, slanting the carpet upward and away. "But it leaves us with a problem. How are we going to get close enough to anybody to ask questions, looking the way we do?"

"What need of question?" asked Belphegor. "I have given you the direction general; you have but to wait for night, then put this strange steed of yours aloft and to its pace, seeking for that ring of flame around the castle."

Shea glanced down to be sure he was following the road. "It isn't just finding the place," he said. "We've got to consider tactics, too. Duke Astolph is somewhere around with that damn hippogriff, and this thing's slow freight by comparison. I don't want to be enchanted down in flames, especially with you aboard, kid."

"Grammercy for your thought of me, fair sir," said the girl: "but I charge you that while we keep this quest, you shall no longer treat me as a woman *par amours*, but as a full companion."

The words were sharp enough, but did he imagine it, or had she said them in a tone anything but sharp? There was not time to make a decision, for peering over the carpet's leading edge, Shea caught sight of a little fan of detritus at the side of a mountain which might be a mine entrance. "I'm going to land there," he told the others. "Belphebe—that is, Belphegor, suppose you go first and smooth out anyone inside."

The carpet slanted smoothly down to a landing in front of the mineshaft, which did not appear to be a mineshaft after all when one got close to it. As Shea stood up to stretch cramped muscles a man appeared at the low entrance. He was old, he was whiskery, and a dirty brown robe was gathered around his waist by a piece of cord.

For a moment he looked at the visitors with widening eyes, then took a step backward, and planting his feet firmly, lifted his right hand with two fingers upraised: "In the name of St. Anthony and the Virgin Mary," he said in a high voice, "depart, cursèd enchantments!"

Shea felt the muscles of his face relax into different patterns and reached a hand up to find that his tusks were gone. He looked at Medoro; the poet had lost his, too.

"Nothing to worry about, Father," he said to the old man. "We're really not enchantments ourselves, just had some put on us, and we're looking for directions."

The old man beamed. "Surely, surely, my son. There be many great and good men of your race, some of whom draw nigh unto God, though in strange wise. And all respect the hermit who has nought but his poverty. Whither wish you to go?"

"Castle Carena," said Shea, the thought flashing through his mind that even if this were the holiest hermit in Spain, his protestation of poverty was laid on with a trowel.

"By the road before you, my children. Over the next pass lies the valley of Pau; beyond it, the village of the same name, wherein stands the church of St. Mary of Egypt, whose vicar is an Austin friar. Beyond that again, a fork in the route—"

"Uh-huh," said Shea. He turned to Belphegor. "That must be the valley where my partner went hunting for Roger just before I met you and Duke Astolph." He turned back to the hermit. "Have you seen any Christian knights going in that direction?"

The old man's face took on a troubled expression. "Nay, children," he said. "I know naught of warlike men or their contentions. These be vanities, even as gold."

Medoro plucked Shea's sleeve. "Of a truth," he said, "there is no truth in this man, and he has evidently seen more than he has told. Let us question him more nearly," He fondled the hilt of his dagger.

Out of the corner of his eye Shea saw Belphegor's fine features take on a look of distaste. He said: "Nothing doing. You don't know Christian hermits, Medoro. Roughing them up only makes them more obstinate, and besides, it wouldn't look good. Anyway, now we're rid of those jann disguises we can find out what we want to know anywhere. So long."

He flipped a hand at the hermit, who lifted his two fingers again and said: "The blessing of God on you, my son."

The three took their places on the carpet and Shea recited:

> "By warp and by woof,
> High over the roof
> Of mountain and tower
> You shall fly in this hour."

Nothing happened.

Shea repeated the verse, and then tried several variations in wording. Still no result. The hermit smiled benignly.

The girl said: "Methinks I can unriddle this, Sir Harold. This religious has not only blessed us, but pronounced an exorcism against enchantments, so that whatever virtue the carpet possessed by your magic is departed, nor may return in his presence. 'Tis not the first such wonder of holy men, nor the last, belike."

"Are you a holy man?" asked Shea.

The hermit folded his arms complacently. "In my humble way, my son, I strive to lead the sinless life."

"Oh, Lord!" said Shea. "Now I suppose we'll have to walk."

Said the hermit: "It were better for your soul to mortify the flesh by walking a thousand miles with bleeding feet than to travel at ease for one."

"No doubt," said Shea, "but right now there are a couple of things more important to me than my soul, and one of them is getting a good friend of mine out of a jam." He was talking over his shoulder as he unbound Roger's legs and made a loop in the knotted turbans to serve as a halter.

Something made a gruesome noise in the cave. Shea cocked his head. "You got an ass, Father?"

The old man's complacency gave way to a look of apprehension. "You would not rob me of my stay and sole companion, my son?"

"No. I told you we were on the square. I just wondered if you'd be interested in selling him."

With surprising alacrity the hermit disappeared into the shaft, to return presently with the ass; a big, tough-looking animal that would help them a good deal in the marching that evidently lay ahead. Shea asked how much; the hermit replied that the service of God could hardly be accomplished on less than five bezants, a figure at which Belphegor made a little round O of her mouth.

Shea felt at his belt, then remembered that the innkeeper had picked him clean and he had forgotten to repossess the money. "Damn," he said. "You got any money, Medoro?"

The Moor spread his hands. "Oh, my lord and brother, had I but a piece of copper, it were at your service. But it was ordained that my monies should be left in my casket, which is in the camp of the Commander of the Faithful, the blessed."

"Hm," said Shea. "Okay, then, let's have one of those bangles," indicating Medoro's jewelled bracelets.

Medoro looked sour. "It is not to be concealed, O friend Harr, that such a jewel is worth a dozen such vile, scrawny beasts as that which stands before us. Has not your Nazarene imam pronounced that gold is vanity to him?"

"That's his risk," said Shea, folding the carpet into a saddle-pad and slinging it on the back of the animal.

"It will be devoted to the increase of holiness," said the hermit, unbinding the rope around his waist and helpfully installing it as a cinch. Shea turned to Roger, who had not said a word: "Okay, big boy, you get the ride."

The direct address seemed to touch off a spring within whatever nest of complexes served the big man for a brain. "Vile cozener!" he shouted. "May Allah descend on me if I separate your bones not one from another. Yet since you do me at least the honor to give me the better place, I will accord it in my mercy that you die before these others, Alhamodillah!"

"Nice of you," said Shea, firmly, tying Roger's feet together under the animal's belly. "But that's not quite the idea. It's just that you're less likely to get loose and massacre us while you're in this position."

They set out. The track had never been intended for wheeled traffic and was so narrow that no more than two could go abreast, a distinctly less comfortable method of travel than the flying carpet. Shea took the lead, one hand on the ass' rope. It was an hour later when he held up a hand to halt the others. "People ahead," he said.

Belphegor came up to join him, bow bent and arrow nocked. The people turned out to be three asses, biting the tops off weeds at the cliff-side and a stout, weather-beaten man, sitting in the shade and resting. The man scrambled up at their approach, hand to knife, then relaxed as Shea said: "Good morning, mister. How's business?"

"Peace and good luck to you, friend," said the man. "Business have I none at the moment, but count that at sundown I shall have much; for look you, I am bound for Pau, where they are holding an auto-da-fe on a paynim sorcerer the day beyond tomorrow. Now that is thirsty work; and I have the wine to slake it." He gestured toward the asses, and Shea perceived that they were laden with skin bags that gurgled liquidly.

Shea thought of Votsy and Dr. Chalmers and didn't quite like the sound of that "paynim sorcerer." But before he could question further, Belphegor burst out: "No more on this. Behold, Medoro, why I still love the free wildwood, when men will still do such things to each other. Have you other tidings, sirrah?"

"Why, not such as you would name tidings, now that you ask," said the man, unabashed. "A small thing only, that will serve as a tale when tales are told. If I were a timorous man, the tale would doubtless be longer and have an unhappy ending, but—"

Belphegor's foot tapped.

"To make a long matter short, as I was taking the short route over the mountain from Doredano, I was set upon by flying demons with horns and great tusks—doubtless a sending of that same sorcerer who will be so finely cooked to-morrow. Had I not fought my way through the press with this single blade, you would not see me here and I should have lost my profit. 'Ware them on the way. To what lord do you take your prisoner?"

"We're taking him to a lady," said Shea, firmly. "He has four black children and won't pay alimony. But she'll probably need a bodyguard who isn't afraid of anything, and we'll tell her you applied for the job. So long."

Heedless of Roger's howls of anger, he set out again.

It took them all day to reach the pass. The rests at Medoro's request became more and more frequent, and he finally developed a blister, which had to be examined by Belphegor, to Shea's intense disgust. She pronounced the infliction so bad that he would have to ride, and this time there was nearly a quarrel, Shea insisted on the danger from the big man's strength and skill with weapons, the girl equally insistent that Medoro was a third of their fighting strength and they would be in poor shape against any attack if he were eliminated.

She won, of course; Medoro mounted the ass, while Roger's feet were unbound and Shea made a slip-noose of turban for his neck, so that any sudden jerk would cut off the big man's wind. They declared a kind of tacit truce; Shea began to talk to him, and for a time wished he hadn't, since the only thing Roger wanted to discuss was broken heads and spilled guts. In desperation he turned to the subject of Bradamant, which had previously produced so strange an effect on the big bruiser. The effect was all that could be asked. Roger looked at the ground and tittered.

"What's she like?" asked Shea. "I've never seen her."

Roger appeared to be undergoing an internal revolution. Finally, with a masterful effort, he produced: "There is no blessedness but in Allah and his Prophet. Her arms are like ash-trees and her buttocks like full moons. Should chance bring union between us, I will contest with you in arms in celebration. But it is to be remarked that your death will not make me master of your Frankish slave-girl with the ill-omened hair; for I would liefer consort with the uttermost daughters of Eblis."

The tables were neatly turned, decided Shea, and let well enough alone till they had crossed the pass and a mile or two down found a camping spot beside a stream. It was not yet twilight, but Belphegor declared that there would be little chance of game later, so she and Medoro went off hunting, while Shea built a fire.

Half an hour later they came back laughing, with four rabbits. She displayed her well-remembered skill at skinning and cooking them; Shea thought he had never tasted anything better, nor for that matter seen anything more pleasant than the spectacle of Medoro inserting morsel after morsel of meat into Roger's mouth, which the latter gulped with a rapidity that suggested he was trying to snap the fingers off.

After the meal, all felt better; Roger almost genial in spite of the fact that he had to be led behind a bush, and Medoro positively brilliant. He improvised comic rhymes; he effectively parodied Dardinell's parade-ground manner; he did a superb imitation of Atlantès working a complicated spell, including his dismay when the spell produced the wrong results. It came close enough so Shea laughed loud and carefree—whereupon Medoro suddenly went serious.

"Lord Harr," he said, "now that your breast is broadened, I would seek unto your advice, as that of an uncle or a learned man in the law. According to the most excellent book of the Prophet of God, on whose name be grace, which is the Book of the Cow, it is lawful for a Muslim to take unto wife what woman he desires. Yet it is written also that one wife is insufficient, whereas two quarrel with each other, and if there be three, the two will combine against the third, so that there is no safety but in a fourth. Yet this woman whom I would wed will have me as single wife only."

Shea smiled wryly. A delicious question to ask him! However, he thought, let's roll with the punch. He said: "It's a tough case. If you marry her that way, you violate your religion, and if she marries you any other way, she violates whatever religion she has, if any. I suggest you both become Zoroastrians. That can't be far from either one."

Belphegor said: "Who be these Zo-ro-astrans?" She tumbled over the word.

"Oh, they seem to have a pretty sound theology, for my money. They hold the existence of equal and opposed powers of good and evil, Ormazd and Thriman. Gets around the difficulty of the doctors of theology. If good is omnipotent, how come there's evil?"

Said the girl: "'Tis not far—" and stopped at the gasp of horror from Medoro.

His mouth was flapping open and shut, rather like that of a carp in a pool. When he found words, it was to say: "The Ghebers! To be a fire-worshipping alchemist! Why, they are filthy cannibals, who dance naked and eat the limbs of human beings! Why, I'd not union with the Queen of the Diamond Isles, had she all wisdom and the bed-arts of the Ethiopians, were she a Gheber! Nay, were she the most beauteous of mortal women to outward seeming, I would know her for the foulest of harlots by such token, who dined only on broiled rats' bones and hired negro slaves to do her service."

Belphegor drew in a long breath. "My Lord Medoro," she said, "that is somewhat ungentle of you. I would pray you to think more deeply on't while we make our couches." She was on her feet, all one graceful movement. "I'm for a tree."

Next morning they breakfasted on the proceeds of the girl's hunting, Medoro slightly querulous over the lack of salt and Roger grumbling that there was no Imam to call the proper hour of prayer. Shea said: "The way I figure it out, I doubt whether we can make the castle today, unless we get some animals to carry us in Pau."

Medoro looked at the girl. "By Allah, if we reach that castle never, it were soon enough for me, unless there be a good Kazi with witnesses there to marry us at once."

Shea opened his mouth, but the girl beat him to it. "Nay, fair Medoro," she said, "let us think not so fast on marriage. For behold, I am as bound by my plighted word as ever knight was, to stand by Sir Harold till this quest be fully accomplished. Whatever faith holds, one must keep faith."

The dampening of Medoro's spirits was only temporary. By time they were ready to start, he was gay and cheerful again, and when Shea led Roger to the ass with the intention of repeating the previous day's arrangement, the poet darted ahead and mounted it at once.

"Hey!" said Shea. "You had your turn yesterday. Now look here—"

Medoro looked down from his seat. "Now Allah burn my liver if I ride not this ass today," he said. "O, son of shame—"

Smack! It was a long reach but Shea landed right on the side of the jaw and Medoro landed with a plunk on the ground. He heaved himself up on one elbow as Shea looked at his own tingling knuckles, wondering what had made his own temper depart to the region where the woodbine twineth.

When he raised his eyes Belphegor was between them, hand on her little belt-knife. "De Shea," she said, in a grating voice, "this passes bearing; a most vile peasantish discourtesy. You are no more my knight, nor I your lady, till you make full apology, nor will I hold communion with you else."

Medoro rode the ass. Shea, trudging along in the dirt and stones, with his hand on Roger's halter, wondered whether the light of his life were exactly bright.

Proceeding grumpily under the pillar of disagreement that kept them all silent, they were still well short of Pau when afternoon drew in and Belphegor announced shortly that if they were to sup, she would have to hunt. This time Medoro did not accompany her, but as he got down from the ass, he suddenly shaded his eyes against the sun and pointed:

"Inshallah!" he said. "Lord Harr, look on a marvel. That tree is surely of peach, such as they have in the land of Circassia, and as the Prophet is the Witness, we shall have fruit to our repast." He skipped off with no sign of blister or limp and in a few moments was back with his arms full of ripe peaches.

It was at that moment that inspiration descended on Harold Shea. "Sit down and take care of Roger while I prepare them for eating," he said. Medoro wrinkled his eyes round a glance that might have been one of suspicion. "Listen, take it easy," said Shea. "I'm sorry I got sore at you this morning."

The poet's face broke out in a beatific smile. "Of a truth, Lord Harr, it is said that the Franks are in fury uncontrollable; but if one bear with them, in friendship generous." He took the slip-knot turban and led Roger to one side.

Shea took off his helmet, stuck it in the ground on its spike; it made a magnificent punchbowl. Four of the peaches went into it. Shea scratched the letters C, H and O with his knife-point on the remaining peaches and arranged them as Doc Chalmers had done which he so unexpectedly produced the Scotch whiskey in Faerie. Accident that time, Shea told himself, but this time whatever happened would be on purpose. He leaned over the helmet and with one eye cocked in the direction where Medoro was rather languidly holding to Roger's noose as the latter recounted one of his tales of assault and battery, repeated softly what he could remember of Doc's spell:

> "So frequently as I with present time
>   The earlier image of our joy compare,
> So frequently I find our less than prime,
>   And little joy than that we once did share:
> Thus do I ask those things that once we had
>   To make an evening run its magic course,
> And banish from this company the sad
>   Thoughts that in prohibition have their source:
> Change, peaches! From the better to the worse."

For a moment he had the dreadful fear that this would give him a mess of rotten peaches, but when he opened his eyes, the helmet was brimmed to overflowing with a golden liquid in which peach-pits and deflated peachskins floated. Shea fished one of the latter out and tasted the surplus. It was peach brandy all right, of a magnificent flavor, and now that he caught it at the back of his palate, a potency rarely equalled in his own cosmos—about 120 proof, he would judge.

"Hey!" he called. "Bring him over here, Medoro. I've made some peach sherbet for you."

The poet got to his feet, jerking the prisoner along. He leaned over the helmet and sniffed. "By Allah, it has a noble perfume, Lord Harr. You are the best of shah-bands; but it should be cooled with snow for fair sherbet."

"I'll trot right over to one of the mountains and get some," said Shea.

Medoro knelt and thrusting his face down to the edge of the helmet, took a long pull. "Allah!" he said. "Of a truth, snow is sorely needed, for this sherbet burns like fire. If this be poison—" he glared at Shea.

"Then I'll be poisoned, too," and Shea took a drink for himself. It certainly did warm the gullet going down.

"Give me some of this sherbet, I pray, in the name of Allah," begged Roger. Shea cautiously disengaged the spike of the helmet from the ground and held it for him, as he took a sip, then a drink.

When he lifted his face from the cup, Medoro said: "Oh lord and brother blest and to profit increased, I would have more of your Frankish sherbet; for the eve is chill, and it does provide a warmth interior."

The helmet went round, and then again, Shea not stinting when it came his turn. Belphegor's anger with him began to fade a little into the background. She'd get over it as soon as she realized her real identity, and he could think of a dozen, twenty, thirty schemes to produce that desirable result, only requiring slight details to be filled in. He could take care of that any time; in the meanwhile, Medoro was one of the most fascinating conversationalists he had ever met, and even Roger was not so bad a guy when you got to know him. The Saracen paladin was telling a tale of his adventures in Cathay, which Medoro was weaving into a ballad of immensely complicated rhythm-scheme, but he kept missing the rhyme at the third line of each stanza, and Shea was correcting him when Belphegor suddenly stood in the center of the little group, a brace of black-plumed birds in her hand.

Medoro looked up, and his mouth fell open. "Now may Ifrits remove me to the outermost depths of the sea an I futter not this damsel," he shouted, and lurched half way to his feet, then sat down. His brows contorted with effort; he tried to get up again and made it. Belphegor dropped the birds.

"I love you for your exceeding loveliness and surpassing beauty," said Medoro, "and you shall grant me the desire of the body, as Ali bin-Hayat says:

"Men craving pardon will uplift their hands;
Women pray pardon with their legs on high:
Out on it for a pious, prayerful work!
The Lord shall raise it in the depths to lie."

He giggled at the girl's horror-filled face, hiccupped, spread his arms and ran at her.

Smack! Medoro sat down abuptly. Shea cried triumphantly: "A most vile peasantish discourtesy!"

The young Moor heaved himself up again, his handsome features contorted. "By Allah!" he said. "You foulest of tribades and filthiest of harlots, that would reject the love of one of the house of Hassan for base-born negroes! Farewell! I seek the camp where there are boys a thousand times lovelier and more faithful." Before any of them could guess his intention, he took three staggering steps to the ass, was on its back and belaboring it to a gallop in the direction whence they had come with his scabbarded scimitar.

Belphegor stood at gaze a second, then snatched up her bow and sent an arrow after him—too late.

"Shurr Harol'," said Roger with owlish gravity, "ish even as I have shaid. Thish red Frankish hair ish ill-omened. You had better be drowned in the shee if you sell not that slave."

Shea ignored him to take the helmet over to Belphegor. "Here, take a drink of this," he said.

She gave him a long, slow glance and accepted the offer with slightly trembling hands. The shaking quieted. "My thanks and good grace to you, Sir Harold," she said, "for I perceive that it is to you I owe this. It is like—like—" She seemed to flounder for a lost memory.

Shea said: "In Latin they would say *In vino veritas.*"

"Oh, aye. Taunt me not; I should have seen him with clear eyes when he would have left you in the tent or put the hermit to the torture. A niggeling and wittold does not make himself a true man with a lute and fair words.

She sat down and pressed the palms of both hands to her eyes. Shea sat beside her and put an arm round her shoulders, but she shook him off. From the background Roger croaked: "Flee away from thish ill-omened wench."

Shea could not be sure whether she was crying or not, and his heart turned flip-flops as he tried to think of something to do. He wished he had not drunk so much of the peach brandy; there seemed to be a haze between him and what he was trying to think.

The hands came down and Belphegor turned a woebegone face toward him. "Nay, the fault's my own," she said, in a flat voice, "and you have been my true knight that would have saved me from a villain. Heigh-ho!" She sighed and stood up. "It falls dusk and we must sup soon if we're to take the road of our quest tomorrow. Nay, no hand-kissing; I'll not have these empty courtesies."

CHAPTER 15

THEY CAME DOWN A HILL TOWARD PAU through the morning light. "I suppose we could get some horses there," remarked Shea, gazing at the range of thatched roofs. "Has nobody any money? I'm broke, and we haven't got Medoro with his gold bracelets."

Belphegor laughed. "Not a groat, I. To those of the woodland seed 'tis the forbidden thing."

Shea looked at Roger. "O man," said the paladin, "know that the hardest of riding is better than the easiest footgoing, as says Al Qa'saf. But as for money, what need? You have a sword to take or magics to make as does my uncle Atlantès when he would have money."

Shea gazed at Roger in astonishment. It was about the first time he had ever heard the big man express an idea, and for a wonder, it seemed a fairly good one. The only trouble was that he had a little less than no idea what type of spell would produce money. The passes, yes—one could manage those—but the psychosomatic element?

Well, one could only try. A hundred yards or so back a bank had caved in on a deposit of fine golden sand. He scooped up a double handful of this, laid it on a handkerchief and tied the corners together. Then he laid the improvised pouch on the ground and traced out a pair of interlacing pentacles, like those on the doors of Atlantès' room in Castle Carena. Belphegor was watching him, and it disturbed him slightly.

"Take this guy a little way off and cover him, will you?" he asked. "Don't let him watch."

The spell—ah, yes, of course, good old Kipling. He chanted:

"Iron's for the soldier, silver for the maid,
Copper for the craftsman, working at his trade.
Sand is but silly stuff, sifting to a fall;
But gold, red gold! is the master of them all."

The handkerchief sagged and looked lumpy. Shea picked it up and heard a gratifying clink within. "All right," he called. "I guess we're set now."

The approaches to Pau seemed curiously deserted, the brown-and-green fields vacant of working men, no women and children at the doorways. Shea puzzled over it until he recalled what the wine-merchant had said about the auto-da-fé, and felt a sudden need for haste. But just at that moment a clanging sound came to his ears, and across the street he perceived a village smith, hammering away at an open-air anvil.

Shea led his prisoner over, and greetings were exchanged. "Where is everybody today?" he asked.

The smith jerked a thumb. "Down the road. Saint's shrine," he said shortly. "Auto-da-fé for the monster. Can't waste time myself." He hefted his hammer, in evident desire for them to be gone so he could carry on with his job. Shea thought these Basques a singularly uncommunicative lot. Nevertheless, he tried again:

"Monster? What monster?"

"Devil. Looks like a wolf. Caught in a wolf-net."

That would be Votsy, all right. The need for hurry was becoming acute, but horses would help. "We'd like to buy horses." He jingled the handkerchief of money.

The lines round the smith's eyes wrinkled craftily. "Have some," he said. "Come, see."

"I don't think I need to. You see, we're rather in a hurry with this prisoner, and we can get any money we spend back from the baron where we're taking him."

Suspicion mingled with the craft. The smith was clearly not used to dealing with customers who bought without asking the price. "Ten bezants," he said, flatly.

"Okay," said Shea. "Lead them out." He opened up his handkerchief-purse and produced a handful of bright gold pieces. As they touched the anvil, however, they instantly changed to little pinches of sand. The smith looked at them and then at Shea. "What's this?" he demanded.

Shea could feel a flush creeping up his face. "Ha, ha, just a joke," he said hollowly, and reaching into the pile, selected another handful to hand them to the smith. But suspicion had now completely gained the upper hand in the man. He rang each piece on the anvil, or tried to, for as soon as metal touched metal, these too dissolved into little cones of sand.

"Scoundrel! Cheat! Magician!" bellowed the man, gripping his hammer in both hands. "Out! Out! Ha, priest!"

Fortunately, he did not offer to pursue as the three beat a hasty retreat. Too late, on the road again, Shea remembered that Kipling's original poem had made iron, not gold, the master of them all, so that of course the spell had gone sour. It did not help matters any that even with the halter around his neck, Roger was snickering.

Shea turned toward the girl. "Look," he said. "This hasn't anything to do with the job we're working on—" he glanced at Roger "—but I think a friend of mine is in trouble. Would it put you out too much to speed up the works?"

For answer she actually smiled at him. "Lead on," she said, and taking one of the arrows from her quiver, prepared to urge Roger to speed; but then: "Hold. Here's one that weeps and may not, for chivalry, be neglected."

Shea turned. With her back toward him and feet in the ditch that bordered the road, there was indeed one that wept. Her back hair was neatly ordered and her figure was young, which lent a certain predisposition toward relieving her distress. As the three halted beside her, she turned a face definitely pretty, though tear-streaked and somewhat dirty, toward them. "They—they—they seek to slay my sweetheart," she got out, before dissolving in another torrent of sobbing.

Belphegor said: "Sir Harold, whatever else you be charged with, here is a quest that turns all quests aside; a woman unjustly in trouble, to wit."

"I don't know about the unjustice," said Shea. "But let's see." He addressed the weeping girl. "Who's they? You mean the people who are holding the auto-da-fé on the monster?"

"Aye. No more monster than me. Am I a monster?" She spread her arms and Shea noticed that her dress was low cut in front.

"Marry, tears mend no torn bodices," said Belphegor, just a trifle acidly.

"The—the priest t-t-took him down to the Saint's cross for burning. Save him!"

Shea hesitated, then looked at Belphegor. The girl was

frowning, but she said strictly: "Sir Harold, meseems that her plaint would be of that friend you bespeak."

"I'm afraid so," he said. "You take—no, you'll need both hands for the bow, and I only need one for the sword. Giddy-ap, Roger." He unsheathed the blade; the girl who had been doing the weeping tagged along behind.

The road turned a shoulder and slanted up a hillside from which figures were visible, moving against the skyline. One or two people turned round, but nobody seemed in the least curious about the spectacle of a Saracen and a red-headed bow-girl leading a monstrous warrior by a noose. As he topped the rise and pressed forward, Shea saw why. The road here ran along the outer edge of a wide terrace on the side of the mountain. On the innermost edge of the terrace, against the cliff, something had been carved which looked rather like a phallic symbol with a halo round its head. In front of this singular erection a huge pyre of wood was erected, and around it a hundred or so peasants were crowding.

The wood was burning vigorously, and in its center, bound to a stake by neck and all four legs, was a huge grey wolf. The logs on which it sat were already a bed of hot coals, the flames around it were consuming its bonds, but except for the fact that the wolf had its tongue out and was panting, it seemed utterly unconcerned with the proceedings.

Shea suddenly recalled the spell under which Atlantès had let Polacek and himself out of the castle's flaming border, and wanted to laugh. Instead he said: "Hello, folks."

Talk died in a circle like ripples spreading from a thrown stone in a pool. A man in a patched black robe, who had been throwing sticks toward the center of the fire, turned and came toward him, blinking with near-sightedness.

"What goes on, Father?" asked Shea.

The priest produced a cross and began to mumble. "Oh, that's all right," said Shea. "I'm not a Saracen, and anyway I'm a friend of the hermit of the mountain." He indicated his prisoner. "See? We've captured Roger of Carena."

The priest studied the prisoner's face, pressing his own close. Roger hawked and spat, but only succeeded in adding another spot on the patched gown. The priest came toddling back toward Shea. "Worshipful sir," he said, "I perceive you are a very mighty man, and I trow, a good Christian. Sir, in your might, perchance you can aid us. Here have we a very demon from the uttermost depths of hell, in monster form, but his master Beelzebub, who is the Lord of Fire, will not permit him to burn."

Shea said: "I'm not sure he's as bad as you think. Had it occurred to you that he might be just a good man under an enchantment?" He stepped forward and raising his voice, addressed the wolf: "Are you Vaclav Polacek?"

The wolf barked twice and nodded vigorously, then raising one paw to emphasize the point, tore away the burned rope that held it. There was a universal "Ooooh" and backward movement in the crowd.

"I thought Doc Chalmers told you to lay off that stuff," said Shea, disgustedly. "Can you get loose?"

"Oow! Ououw! Ouououw!" said the wolf.

"Well, lay off it for a minute, for the love of Mike, till I get you off the hook." He turned toward the priest. "It's like I said. He's a Christian squire under an enchantment. I am Sir Harold de Shea." He did his best to strike an attitude. The priest looked at him with near-sighted skepticism.

"Votsy!" said Shea. "This guy don't believe you're the goods. If those ropes are burned through enough, come over here and lick one of his feet."

"Wrrrower!" howled the wolf, and leaped against his ropes. They gave; there was a universal scream of terror from the assembled peasants and they scattered as the animal came leaping through the flames, throwing burning coals in all directions. The priest stood his ground, but his face was set in tight lines and he was vigorously fingering his rosary as the wolf that was Votsy sat down and licked at his feet. After a moment or two the priest put one hand down and gingerly patted his head, but removed the hand instantly as up the valley, in the direction they were going, a bugle sounded "Rump-te-umpte-um-tum." At least it sounded like a bugle. All the notes were flat.

Everybody gazed. Up the rise came a column of horsemen, headed by three who bore slender spears with dirty pennons of colored wool too heavy for the slow motion of their progress to lift and make clear. Behind them came the bugler, and behind them again, three knights in full plate armor with their helmets banging at their knees. Shea recognized Count Roland d'Aglante and Reinald of Montalban; the third had slightly more delicate features and a surcoat over his mail divided red and white across the middle, with a huge gold buckle occupying the center. They were followed by a score or more of mounted men-at-arms in iron hats with brims and mail-shirts of over-lapping metal scales. His eyes were torn from the sight by an inarticulate burp from Roger, who suddenly seemed to have difficulty with his breathing, though the halter had not been pulled tight,

There was no point in trying to conceal anything, Shea stepped boldly to the center of the road and, holding his hand up like a traffic cop, said: "Hey!"

The bugle gave a toot, and the riders pulled up. Reinald cried: "'Tis the turban-knight! How hight he—Sir Harold de—du Chaille? No matter. Hail, fair Belphegor!"

"Regard!" said the knight in the surcoat, in a high voice. "Roger of Carena, and in bonds. This may not be borne!" The knight vaulted down and Shea realized that "he" was a handsome, brown-haired woman of show-girl size. She whipped a dagger from her belt. Roger was apparently trying to use one of his feet to dig a hole to fall into, his gaze fixed on the ground. Shea thrust himself between the two. "Listen," he said, "this guy's my prisoner."

Count Roland looked down from his horse benignly. "My lady and fair cousin Bradamant, peace; for this is good law. This young sir is a dubbed knight, Sir Harold de Shea, to wit, and if he holds Lord Roger bound it is by right of fair conquest."

"Then I challenge him!" said Bradamant, picking at her belt for a pair of gloves. "For this is my very soul and love and I will assay all desperately upon the body of any who holds him. Lord Reinald, be my aid."

"Cut them down!" said Reinald harshly.

Roland leaped down from his own horse, clanging like an earthquake in a kitchen. "Then must I even stand his, to make the balance fair; for this is a very gentle knight that has done me much service. Ho, Durandal!" He lifted up a great cross-hilted sword, and Belphegor drew back a couple of steps, snatching an arrow from her quiver and bending her bow—not at Bradamant but at Roger. Shea admired his wife's presence of mind, even if the mind was not entirely her own. Reinald looked black, but Bradamant checked her rush, and gave a little laugh.

"Nay, gentles," she said, "let us not fall on contention when Saracen banners be over the next crest, but dissolve this in amical agreement. Sir Harold, my hand." She put the dagger back and extended it.

Shea reached out and took it. "Okay, lady," he said. "My story is that I need this guy in my business. A friend of mine is in Castle Carena and can't get out, because Atlantès has built a wall of fire around it, and unless I deliver Roger there it's no dice."

"Ah, but—" said the lady warrior "—this is my more than friend and most dear love." She waved a hand at Roger, who said "Allah!" under his breath. "Surely, it is less than knightly to keep us one from the other."

"Yet even more so," said Belphegor, putting her arrow back and stepping forward in evident enjoyment of the prospect of a legal argument, "—were he to fail his duty to his vavassour and liege lord who is held prisoner."

"Ah, but the greater wipes out the less," said Bradamant. "In making deliverance of Lord Roger to this Saracen, Sir Harold would fail in duty to the Emperor Charles, who is liege lord to us all."

"Not to me," said Shea.

The three knights gasped, and Roland's face went a trifle grim. "Sir knight," he said, "a truce to profitless discourse. You know me for your friend; will you hear my judgment in this cause?"

Shea looked at the surrounding men-at-arms. Might as well put a good face on it, especially as Roland didn't seem to be a bad guy. "Sure," he said, "anything you say is all right with me."

"And you, my lady Bradamant?"

"That will I."

"Then hark." Roland unslung his big sword from his belt and kissed the hilt. "This is my judgment, given in honor, as the holy St. Michael stands my aid: that Sir Harold de Shea release the Lord Roger to the Lady Bradamant. But since she has the ring that daunts all enchantments, she shall forthwith take oath to rescue Sir Harold's lord from durance in Castle Carena. This deed I lay on her; and none other shall be accomplished till it be done."

Belphegor clapped her hands. "Oh, well thought on!" she said. Bradamant's face also expressed pleasure. She stepped to her horse, produced a sword almost as large as Roland's and held it out to him. He lifted the hilt up before her;

she kissed it and extended one hand: "I swear it," she said, and turned to Shea. "Now handsell me your prisoner."

"What do I do?" he asked.

"Place his hand in mine."

"I can't. He's tied up."

"Loose him, want-wit!" She stamped her foot.

Shea was not sure this was a good idea, but nobody else seemed to have any objections, so he stepped around behind the big man, and untied some of the knots, then as Roger gave an explosive sigh of relief, took one of his hands and laid it in Bradamant's.

"Do you assign me all rights of war and ransom in this man?" she asked.

"Sure."

"Then I receive him." She dropped Roger's hand, and with a roundhouse swing, hit him a terrific slap on the side of his face. "Come, varlet!" Roger slowly lifted a numbed arm, and then, instead of hitting her back, surprisingly began to titter. "You accompany us to Carena."

Roger's face straightened out. "O my lady, I pray you, take me not back thither, where mine uncle will coop me up like a chicken."

"Tish! have I not the ring, which is proof against all that he can do? Sir Harold, will you ride with us?"

"Sure," said Shea. He looked around.

The wolf that was Vaclav Polacek was nowhere to be seen.

CHAPTER 16

SHEA THOUGHT RAPIDLY. BRADAMANT COULD probably be trusted to keep her word, and even if she couldn't, there was no particular immediate danger to Doc and Florimel. But the danger to Vaclav was both immediate and particular. If they captured him again, someone was almost certain to think of strangling or using a silver weapon instead of the fire that failed. Very likely they would get him, too. He turned to the others:

"I think you could operate better at Castle Carena without us," he said. "There's a friend of mine in trouble, and I'm afraid I've got to do something about it. Bel—Belphegor, it's the sweetheart of that girl. Will you come along?"

She put two fingers to her lips. "'Tis not in our compact. But—aye, that will I. Whither go we?"

"My guess would be that he'd be looking for that girl. Maybe we ought to go back to about where we found her."

"Think you he would return by the village where so late they'd have burned him?"

"You have something there, kid. Votsy is as nutty as a fruit-cake, but I think he'd be bright enough to cut around the back way."

"Come, then," said the girl. "I know some little of woodland trails." She turned to the paladins. "Gentles, I salute you farewell till a happier meeting."

The armored men raised their hands, the bugle blew again and the group broke up. A horse had been brought for Roger; Shea noticed that as he and Bradamant rode off in the direction of Castle Carena they were holding hands and not giving any particular attention to their route. In their condition, he wondered how good they would be at the business of getting Doc out of Castle Carena.

Behind the shrine the ground dipped sharply, then rose up a bank set with low bushes to the veritable forest beyond.

Belphegor's eyes swept it from side to side: "Thither lies his slot," she said, pointing.

Shea could see nothing that looked like a trail, but when he plunged across the declivity at the girl's heels and up the other side, there was a broken branch on one of the bushes, and beyond, where she waved a hand, the mark of a wolf's pad, deeply impressed on the soft ground.

"Hey," he said, "wouldn't we save time by short-cutting along the road?"

She turned a laughing face. "Nay, who'd go roadwise when they could walk the free way of the forest? And more— it is the nature of the wolfish kind to be somewhat scatter-wit in purpose. Trust me, we shall come on him the sooner by following direct. See, there turned he to the left."

She went more rapidly than Shea would have believe possible. The sun slanted down through the leaves in speckled patterns and occasionally a bird chirped or dipped and swooped away before him. His Saracen costume was not exactly what he would have chosen for the occasion, but he found himself suddenly happy.

Belphegor hummed a little air to herself as she examined some markings at the side of another little clump of bushes. "Here he turned aside to strike at some small game," she announced. "A rabbit, belike. And here he lay to rest after the pursuit. We gain; press on."

She was tireless; it was he who had to ask for the first halt, and later, for another. Toward what he judged to be noon they made the third pause by the side of a little stream from which they drank and shared half one of the birds left from the previous night's supper. The girl frowned suddenly.

"Sir Harold," she said, "it is passing strange, but me-seems there is in this something familiar and not unsweet, as though all this were a twice-told tale. Yet sure am I that we have never wandered the wildwood together before."

"Oh, yes we—" began Shea and then stopped. No use giving her a jar that might set up a resistance to her re-developing memory. "Do you think we'll find him?" he said instead, changing the subject rapidly.

"Oh, aye, and that soon. Come, let us be afoot again."

She was on her feet in a single graceful motion and they were off. The wolf had certainly done a good deal of circling, either because he couldn't make up his own mind, or perhaps because he had lost his way. Twice more they found places where he had rested, and then, as they passed another brook, the girl pointed suddenly. Shea saw a footprint into which the water was just oozing. He stopped, filling his lungs, and shouting: "Vaclav!"

There was a sound in the underbrush, and the wolf came trotting from behind a tree with his tongue out, shaking his head and bouncing in delight.

Shea said: "What was the matter? Get lost?"

"Arf!" said the wolf.

"Okay, now you're found. Listen here, you prize idiot. You've nearly gummed the works for all of us. Now you stick by us and don't get out of sight. I can handle some magic all right, but I don't understand the higher sorcery well enough to disenchant you, so we'll have to wait till we find Doc. As it is it's damned lucky Atlantès fire-proofed you before you turned into a werewolf again."

The wolf put its tail between its legs and emitted a moan of contrition. Shea turned his back and said to Belphegor: "Can you get us on the road to Castle Carena again?"

"Assuredly. It lies that way." She pointed. "But do you find the woods that are my joy so comfortless?"

"It's not that, kid. We got business. Afterward, we can come back here, if you like, and—oh, what the hell, let's go."

The approach of dusk found them still among trees. While Shea made a fire the wolf, under strict instructions, went to help Belphegor with her hunting, flushing game for her arrow and retrieving it afterward. She came back with five rabbits, two quail and a larger bird of some kind, remarking: "If we keep this adventure, I must even find some means of gaining new arrows. Two were lost on that bout, and though I have some skill as a fletcher, both tools and seasoned wood are wanting."

The evening's bag looked like a lot for three people, but the wolf ate everything they left and looked hungrily for more. Shea was glad that they didn't have much farther to go at this rate. It would wear both of them out to feed the confounded animal.

The sun was already high in the morning when they came out on the track, a few hundred yards short of the fork where he had separated from Polacek on the outward journey. Now they were on the last lap. The wolf, which had been alternately trotting on ahead and dropping back as though it found their pace unbearably slow, suddenly came tearing up, whining and emitting little sharp howls.

"What's the matter, old man?" asked Shea.

The wolf bounded, stiff-legged, nuzzling Shea's legs and running a few steps back in the direction of Pau.

"Wants us to go back and find that girl, I guess," said Shea. The wolf howled some more, then nipped Shea by the bagginess of his trousers and tried to lead him in the desired direction.

"Listen, I'm not—" began Shea, and then saw what the wolf had been trying to tell him. A column of dust was rising along the track, with heads moving beneath it. Belphegor shaded her eyes, then gave a little squeal. "The Saracens! By the foul fiend, how slipped they past Count Roland? And see—Medoro among them."

"He must have gone over the pass and picked up a party looking for us—or else that damned smith put him on our track," said Shea.

The heads jerked forward in more rapid movement. "They have spied us!" cried Belphegor. "Up yon hill-shoulder! They cannot reach us mounted there, and mayhap we shall gain the shelter of the trees."

The horsemen were coming on fast, about twenty of them. High-pitched yells announced that they had seen their quarry.

Shea and his companion reached the round of the shoulder and pelted through a clump of scrubby oaks. Beyond, a slope of crumbled shale towered over them. They sank in the loose stuff halfway to their knees, every effort to go higher loosening a minor landslide that carried them staggering back. It was like a treadmill.

Below, a couple of horsemen were picking their way through the rocks at the base of the shoulder; others were spreading left and right. An arrow zipped into the shale above Shea's head. He wished he knew some kind of magic that would work quick.

"No use," he said bitterly. "We'll have to stand and try to fight it out." He gripped the girl's hand and ran the few steps back toward the trees.

The Saracens were skirmishing around the base of the shoulder, stopping now and then to yell. A few of them had double-curved bows and were letting off arrows.

Belphegor crouched behind a rock and let off one of her

own shafts at a dodging shape. The shot missed, splintering on a stone behind. The next hit a horse, which reared and threw its rider. Belphegor dodged as half a dozen arrows clattered around her in return.

Medoro was on a fine white horse, well out of range. His voice floated up thinly. "Cease from shooting lest you do her a harm! She shall be taken alive, but I will give five thousand dirhams for the head of the man!"

A man threw up one arm and rolled out of his saddle, an arrow right through his body and tipped with a spurt of blood. The rest drew back, dismounted, and leaving one or two to hold horses, ran at the base of the shoulder with swords and spears.

Out from behind a rock slipped a big grey hairy shape which lit on the back of a Saracen with a long bound. Good old Vaclav! The man went down, screaming, in a voice that was suddenly choked, and Belphegor's bowstring snapped like a harp.

Thump! Down went one of the attackers, clutching his stomach and chewing at the grass. An arrow glanced up and away from the helmet of another. Thump! The leader of the rush was down, with an arrow right through the eye.

"Allahu Akhbar!" screamed Medoro from below. "Ten thousand dirhams!"

A Saracen stopped with an arrow through his forearm. The others set up a discordant yell and came rushing and stumbling up from all sides, clambering over those who had taken the girl's arrows. The wolf got the hindmost by the leg, wolf and man rolling down the hill, the latter squealing with terror as his weapon failed to bite. Belphegor nailed the man with the helmet neatly through the throat.

"My last shaft, Harold," she cried.

Smart girl, he thought, to plant it where it did the most good, and drove his arm forward in a long lunge. The scimitar-like blade was unhandy, but it went right through the open mouth of the man before him. Shea parried a cut with his dagger and swung, but the man had a helmet, which took the blow with a clang, and Shea's blade snapped off at the hilt. However, the blow had force enough to knock the man over backward, and he carried the legs from under a couple of others.

Someone hurled a barb-headed javelin just as Shea recovered from the stroke. The weapon missed and hung

quivering in a tree. Shea and Belphegor grabbed for it together. He reached it first, jerked it loose, snapped it over
his knee, and gripped the pointed end like a rapier. "Get
into a tree," he called to the girl. The Saracens were closing
in fast; Shea had just time to turn around, feint at the
nearest, dodge his swinging cut, and lunge. The point got
him right below the chin.

The next man gave ground, so that Shea's lunge fell short.
He leaped back, barely parrying a cut from the side with
his inadequate blade. They were ringing him, he couldn't
face three ways at once, and was too busy parrying even
for a quick thrust. A blow on the side of the head made his
senses spin; only his helmet kept the edge out.

Then a sound drowned the shouts of the Saracens; a blast
on a horn, deep, full and resonant. It sounded like the horn
of Heimdall that had made the glaciers shake; but this one
had a wild discordant edge that made Shea's skin crawl
and his teeth ache. A dreadful feeling of fear and horror
seized him; he wanted to burst into tears, to get down on
his knees. The horn sounded again, and all at once the
Saracens were bounding down the shoulder, their shouts
changed to cries of panic. Shea almost ran after them.

A shadow floated across the shoulder and he looked up
to see Duke Astolph soaring past through the air on his
hippogriff. He was outlined against the sky as he raised the
horn to his lips once more and blew the Saracens along
the valley.

But not all of them. Shea looked down in time to see a
short, bearded character—who must have been deaf, for
he showed no sign of being affected by the horn—on one
knee, not twenty yards away, drawing a curved bow. As
the man released, Shea ducked almost instinctively and the
arrow went over his head.

A cry made him turn round. Belphegor had reached for
a dropped scimitar, and now she was sinking to her knees,
the arrow sticking in her side.

Shea hurled himself at the Muslim archer, who dropped
his bow and whipped out a short yataghan. For three
seconds their weapons flickered like sunbeams. Shea parried
and drove the javelin-point into the fellow's forearm, where
it stuck between the bones. The man dropped his weapon
and pulled back, tearing the javelin from Shea's grasp.

Shea snatched up the yataghan. His antagonist fell on

his knees and lifted the one good arm. "In the name of Allah! Would you strike a man unarmed?"

"Damn right I would," snarled Shea and did so. The head came off, bounced, bounced again and rolled down the hill.

Shea went back to where Belphegor lay among the rocks, her face pale and her eyes half closed. He took her in his arms.

"Harold," she said.

"Yes, dearest."

"All is crystal clear. I am Belphebe of the woods, daughter of Chrysogonë, and you are my dearest dear."

Shock was often a good cure in amnesia cases. But what the hell good did it do either of them now? He gulped.

"I would have borne your sons," she said faintly. "'Twas a brave match and a joyous."

"It's not as bad as that."

"Aye, I fear me. I go to Ceres and Sylvanus. Kiss me before I go."

He kissed her. The lips smiled wanly and he placed his hand over her heart. It was beating, but slowly and weakly.

She sighed a little. "A brave match . . ."

"What ho!" said a familiar deep voice. Astolph stood over them, the horn in one hand, the hippogriff's bridle in the other. "Oh, I say, is the young lady hurt? That's a bit of too bad. Let me have a look at her."

He glanced at the projecting arrow. "Let's see the pulse. Ha, still going, but not for long. Internal bleeding, that's the devil. Quick, young fellow, get me some twigs and grass and start a fire. I believe I can handle this, but we'll have to work fast."

Shea scrambled around, cursing the slow inefficiency of flint and steel, but getting the fire going. Astolph had drawn an enormous pentacle around them with a stick and had whipped together a tiny simulacrum of an arrow out of a twig, with a bunch of grass representing the feathers. He tossed this in the fire, muttering a spell. The smoke billowed around chokingly, much more than so small a fire had any right to make. Belphebe was invisible.

Shea jumped violently as he observed, beyond the border of the pentacle, a pair of eyes hanging unsupported in the air on a level with his own. Just eyes, with black pupils. Then there were more pairs, sometimes at angles or moving a bit, as though their invisible owners were walking about.

"Stay where you are," said Astolph between spells. His arms were outspread and Shea could see him waving them through the smoke as he chanted in several languages at once.

Something deep inside Shea's head kept saying: Come on out; come out, come out; it's wonderful; we'll make you a great man; come out; just step this way; this will be the greatest thing you've ever known; come with us . . . and something stirred his muscles in a movement toward the eyes. He had taken a full staggering step toward the eyes before he got a grip on himself, and sweat stood on his forehead with the effort of trying to keep from another step.

Suddenly the fire went out, the smoke died as though it had been sucked into the ground and the eyes disappeared. Astolph stood by the ashes, big beads of perspiration on his handsome face. The lines around his mouth were drawn. "Bit of warm work that," he said. "Lucky you didn't put your head outside the pentacle."

Belphebe sat up and smiled. The arrow was gone and there was no trace of where it had pierced the tunic save a big bloodstain down the side.

"I'd jolly well like to fix that for you," said Astolph, "but I'm not exactly a magic laundryman, you know."

"My lord, you have done enough and more than enough," said the girl, getting a little unsteadily to her feet. "I—"

"Bye the bye," interrupted Astolph, "you could do with a bit of leaching yourself, Sir Harold."

Shea realized that he had been wounded. There was blood on his face from the blow the helmet had stopped, a cut on one arm and another on the thigh. All responded readily enough to Astolph's magic, by no means so drastic this time. As the Duke finished his passes, Belphebe reached for Shea's hand:

"So now we are whole and united. Will you forgive the seeming churlishness of one who knew not her own mind?"

"Listen, kid, do I have to answer that?" said Shea, and took her in his arms. Astolph looked down the slope.

CHAPTER 17

AFTER A FEW MINUTES ASTOLPH SAID: "IF you two don't mind, you know, I'd like a word of explanation. I thought it a bit odd when you toddled off together, but—"

Belphebe swung round, with her gay laugh. "Duke Astolph, wit you well that this is my very true and beloved husband; yet save for the wound of which you leached me in such marvellous wise, I had not known it, for I was magicked here in a strange manner by Sir Reed."

"Really? Glad to hear it. Wonderful thing, marriage—increases the population. You might have done worse; he's been a stout fellow." He began counting "—six, seven, eight. You'll want your arrows back, won't you, old girl? Those Saracens have certainly had it. Shouldn't care to take that many on at once myself. Must be something to that sword-play of yours."

"Oh, we had them at a disadvantage," said Shea. "And while you're about accepting our thanks for saving our lives, will you tell us how you happened along so opportunely?"

"Simple matter, really," said Astolph. "I was out scouting. Agramant's on the move, and I daresay we shall have a battle. Too bad we haven't Roger on our side; bad man in a brawl, only Roland can stand up to him. I hear he reached the Mussulman camp."

Shea grinned. "He got out of it, too. I ought to know. I brought him. The last I saw of him, he and Bradamant were on their way to get my friend Sir Reed out of hock."

Astolph's eyebrows wiggled. "Indeed! Jolly good of you, and tit for tat, what? I daresay the Emperor will give you a title. Hello, what's this?"

This was Vaclav Polacek, in the form of a werewolf, who had disentangled himself from one of the bodies on the slope and was coming slowly up the hill. "A werewolf, as I live! Extr'ordin'ry! Doesn't belong in this time-stream at all."

Shea explained, and with a few expert passes, Astolph changed the wolf back into Vaclav Polacek. The Rubber Czech felt his throat. "That last guy nearly strangled me," he complained, "but I got him. And I'm still sore all over from the pounding those peasants gave me with their clubs. Boy, when they let me have it I sure was glad I was the kind of wolf it takes silver to kill."

"But how'd you get into that shape?" asked Astolph. "I know enough magic to be sure lycanthropy isn't exactly a habit with you."

Polacek smiled with embarrassment. "I—uh—I got fed up with walking and I tried to turn myself into an eagle so I could look for Roger better, but I came out a werewolf instead. I guess I made a mistake."

"Rather," said Astolph. "Now look here, young man. I shouldn't try that again, if I were you. It's quite on the cards that you'd make the transformation permanent, and you'd find it deuced embarrassing."

Polacek said: "It nearly was this time. I kept getting the most awful craving for human flesh. Belphebe was in a tree and I couldn't reach her, but you'll never know how close you came to being eaten last night."

Shea gulped. Astolph laughed and said: "I really must buzz off, you chaps. Now that we're well rid of that scouting party, the Emperor will very likely want to use this valley for his main advance. Cheerio! Come, Buttercup." He was off.

"If we're going to run into any more armies, I want some equipment," said Shea. "Come on, Votsy, let's see what we can pick up."

They made their way slowly down the slope, trying various weapons while Belphebe retrieved her arrows and tried, but rejected, some of those the Moors had used in their short bows. At the foot of the slope, the girl put her hand to her mouth.

"My love and lord," she said. "I am much foredone with weariness, and I doubt not it is the same with you. Shall we not rest a space?"

"Yes, let's, but not here, where there are so many stiffs lying around," said Shea.

They moved along the valley, slowly picking their way

across stones, till they reached a spot where a grassy slope slanted down past trees from the left, and stretched out. Polacek said: "The only thing I could want now would be a three-decker sandwich on rye and a cup of coffee. How about it, Harold, could you conjure one up?"

"Might, but it probably wouldn't have any nourishment in it," said Shea with a yawn. "I don't know all about this magic business yet. I wish I knew what made that spell about the jann go wrong. . . ." His voice trailed off. Belphebe's head was nestled in the hollow of his arm.

He thought he had only closed his eyes a minute, but when he opened them Polacek was snoring and the sun was already dropping toward the mountain rim.

"Hey," he said, "wake up, everybody. Company's coming."

It was indeed the sound of hoofbeats that had roused him. Up the valley four riders were visible. As they drew nearer, he recognized Bradamant, Roger, Chalmers and Florimel, the last riding side-saddle. They pulled up before the three at the roadside; there was a general shaking of hands and making of salutations.

Shea said: "I wasn't sure you could make it without help. How did you manage it?"

Said Bradamant: "Sir knight, if knight you be, know that the power of this ring against all enchantments whatsoever is very great. Therefore holding the ring in my mouth and Lord Roger by the hand, it was a light matter to cross so feeble a wizardry as the wall of flame, and thus to draw your companions forth with me. Do I stand acquit of my oath to you?"

"Yep," said Shea. "We're square."

"Then I'm for the north and the Emperor's army with this, my prisoner and new aid."

She motioned at Roger, who tittered again, and wriggled in his saddle so much that he almost fell off.

"Okay," said Shea. "Thanks and so long." He reached up to shake her hand but before the contact was made, there was a flash of light that seemed to split the evening sky and a violent explosion which sent a tall tree by the roadside spraying round the travellers in a fine rain of burned chips.

They turned with a simultaneous gasp to see Atlantès of Carena standing on the stump, outlined in shimmering light and with a wand in his hand.

"Link hands everybody!" said Chalmers, quickly. "He can't hurt us under the protection of Bradamant's ring."

"Vile traitors!" squealed the little magician. "Know that you had already been a thousand times worse than dead but that there stood among you the peerless paladin, the pearl of the age, my nephew. But now that I am near enough to direct my vengeance, you shall no longer escape." He pointed the wand at Chalmers and began muttering a spell. Blue lights flashed around the tip, but nothing happened.

"Better try the other barrel," said Shea. "That one missed fire."

Atlantès stamped and grimaced. "Allah upon me that I should forget the ring of enchantment!" He clapped a hand to his head. "Yet it is said: no victory without some pain of defeat." He began to trace patterns in the air. "Stir you from this spot and you shall receive the reward of your betrayals."

"Hold my hand carefully, Harold," said Chalmers, squatting and reaching with his other hand to trace a circle on the ground round the party. He added other geometrical elements to make a full-grown pentacle, reciting his own spells as he did so.

"There," he said, letting go Shea's hand. "We're safe from him for the time being, though we seem to be besieged. Dear me!"

Atlantès had pointed his wand again, the group felt something rush past them in the air, and a rock on the other side of the road split in a blaze of light. Belphebe placed an arrow on her string.

"I do not believe that will be of any service, young lady," said Chalmers. "I am afraid, Harold, that this gentleman is a much better magician than I, and the most that can be accomplished at present is to accord a certain amount of protection—"

"Maybe I could do something," said Polacek.

"No!" said Chalmers and Shea together. Then the former went on. "However, Harold, you do possess a rather extraordinary skill with the poetic elements in magic. If we were to work together, we might be able to accomplish something."

"I dunno, Doc," said Shea. "We can try, but my spells haven't been going too well in this cosmos." He described what had happened with the growing of the hair on his face and the jann disguises. Beyond the pentacle the sun was behind the peaks. In the long shadows Atlantès was incanting busily and under his wand a swarm of misshapen hobgoblins began to appear among the rocks. Apparently he meant to make a real siege of it.

"Goodness gracious, I am somewhat at a loss," said Chalmers. "You're certain you made the passes correctly, Harold? Hmmm—what was your poetic element?"

Shea described how he had used elements from Shakespeare and Swinburne.

"Oh, I am relieved. The explanation is quite simple. Like all semi-Mohammedan universes, this one is extremely poetic, and since you employed highly inspired poetry, the effect was somewhat beyond your original calculations. This also suggests a means of relief from our present situation. Do you happen to recall any lines from the major poets having to do with motion or progress?"

"How would Shelley do?" asked Shea.

"Quite well, I believe. Are you ready? Very well, suit the rhythm of your recitation to my movements." He began to make the passes with his hands as Shea recited:

"My coursers are fed on the lightning,
    They drink at the whirlwind's stream,
And when the red morning is brightening
    They have strength for the swiftness I deem:
Then ascend with me, children of ocean!"

The result was somewhat unexpected. The four horses on which the party from Carena had come bounded straight into the air as though on springs and before anyone could stop them, leaped at Atlantès' collection of monsters, who scattered in all directions, but not rapidly enough to keep themselves from squashing under the flying hooves like so many tomatoes. Roger whooped with laughter; Chalmers looked a trifle dismayed. "I confess—" he began, and then stopped, looking up.

Against the fading evening sky Duke Astolph on his hippogriff was soaring in to a four-point landing.

He addressed Shea: "Did you summon me, old man? I hope it's important; that children of ocean spell is deuced wracking, but being English I couldn't well resist. Oh, I see; a spot of trouble with our old friend Atlantès."

The proprietor of Carena sneered unpleasantly from outside the pentacle. "O noble and puissant lords, now there is no help for it but that you release to me my beloved nephew, the pearl of Islam. For know that I am of greater power than all magicians of the Franks, save Malagigi alone, and he lies still in durance."

Astolph cocked his head on one side. "Indeed," he said. "Do you want to be released, Roger?"

The pearl of Islam seemed to be having difficulty with his breathing. He looked at the ground, then at Bradamant, then quickly away. "By Allah, nay," he finally managed to get out.

Astolph turned to the enchanter. "Tell you what I'll do, old thing; I'll make you a sporting proposition. I believe Sir Harold's friend here wants his lady to receive human form. I'll take you on in a contest to see who can do it, winner take all, including Roger."

"By Allah, 'tis some Frankish trick," said Atlantès.

"Suit yourself, old man. I can transport them all away from you on Buttercup, you know." He scratched the hippogriff behind the ears.

The magician lifted his hands to heaven. "I am afflicted by the sons of Satan," he wailed. "Nevertheless I will even accept this offer."

Both he and Astolph began making rapid passes. The Duke suddenly vanished, and a mist condensed out of the air around the pentacles, growing and growing until the spectators could no longer see one another. The air was filled with rustlings.

Then the mist thinned and vanished. Florimel had vanished from her own pentacle and stood in that of Atlantès. The latter said: "Behold—" and stopped as Astolph reappeared with a man as tall as himself; a man with a long white beard, neatly combed, and a mane of white hair. He was dressed with formidable correctness in cutaway, pin-striped trousers and spats, with a top-hat at a rakish angle on his head and a pink carnation in his buttonhole.

"Permit me," said Astolph, "to present the Honorable Ambrose Sylvester Merlin, C.M.G., C.S.I., D.M.D., F.C.C. F.R.G.S., F.R.S., F.S.A, and two or three etceteras."

Merlin said in a deep bell-like voice: "That girl's a sham

of some sort. Just a trick, and I'll fetch the right one back."
He whipped a wand out of an interior pocket, traced his
own pentacle and began incanting. Again the mists thickened,
this time shot with little lights.

Five minutes later they cleared and there were two Flori-
mels, identical in dress, pose and appearance.

Merlin calmly slipped his wand in his pocket and stepped
to the nearest girl. "This one's the real one, mine. Are you
not, my dear?" He lifted his plug hat courteously.

"Aye, good sir." She gave a little squeal of pleasure. "And
I do feel that blood, not snow flows in my veins."

Merlin held out a finger. A yellow flame appeared at the
tip, bright in the dusk. He held up Florimel's arm and ran
the flame quickly along it. "Observe. No more reaction than
any normal person." He blew the flame out. "Must be off,
Astolph. That numismatic exhibition at the Phidias Club."

"Many thanks, old man," said Astolph. Merlin vanished.

"Spawn of the accursed!" shouted Atlantès. "Here stands
the veritable Florimel."

Shea noted that Chalmers was making passes. The other
Florimel, the one in Atlantès' pentacle, blinked once or
twice as though just awakened, and turned into the peasant
girl Shea had seen weeping at the roadside near Pau. Polacek
gave a gurk. "Hey, Cassie!" he called.

The girl gave one glance, and leaped for him, crying:
"Oh, my wolfie!"

"I should say that settled the matter," said Astolph. "Come
along, Roger."

"Nay!" said Atlantès. "May my hair turn to scorpions if
I permit this!"

"Ah, but you can hardly prevent it, you know," said the
Duke imperturbably. "Your spells won't hold these people
any more. Laws of magic, you know; you made an agreement and spells to keep from fulfilling it will fail."

"By the seven imps of Satan, sir duke, there was no
agreement that I should not have your head," said Atlantès
and raising his wand, began to incant again. So did Astolph.

Shea touched Chalmers on the shoulder. "Let's get out
of here," he said. "I think there's going to be fireworks."

The three psychologists and their ladies turned their backs
on the disputants and through the falling dark started toward Pau. They had not gone fifty paces when there was a

crack like a cannon-shot and the landscape flashed with electric blue. One of the magicians had thrown a thunder-bolt at the other.

"Hurry!" said Chalmers. They ran. Crack followed crack, merging into a frightful thunder. The earth began to quiver beneath them. A boulder came loose from the hillside and lolloped down past.

As they ran they glanced back over their shoulders. The side of the hill was hidden by a huge, boiling thundercloud, lit from beneath with flashes, and a forest fire was already spreading from its base. A piece of the mountainside came loose and slid. Through the repeated thunderclaps they heard the piercing sound of Astolph's horn.

"My word," said Chalmers, slowing down. "I—ah—per-ceive . . . that some further steps in rejuvenation will be necessary before I can indulge in much more athletics. I should mention, Harold, the reason why Atlantès was so very anxious to detain us. Apparently he has not yet learned the secret of inter-universal apportation, however adept he may be in other respects."

"I bet he never does learn it now," said Shea, a little grimly, looking back to where the battle between the two magicians had now settled down to a mere tornado.

"It would be just as well," said Chalmers.

"Say, you two," remarked Polacek, "while you're speaking about that, what about Walter?"

"Holy smoke!" said Shea. "He's been back there in Xan-adu eating honey for a week and he doesn't like it."

A grin spread slowly over the face of the Rubber Czech. "That isn't all," he remarked. "Remember how long we were in Xanadu? It was hours, though it couldn't have taken Doc more than a few minutes to find out that he'd made a mistake."

"Goodness gracious!" said Chalmers. "Then Walter has been there a month or more. I must certainly address myself to the problem."

"What I want to know," said Shea, "is how we're going to get that cop back to Ohio. But I'm not going to lose any sleep over it."

He squeezed Belphebe's hand.